Hattie's War

Hattie's War

Hilda & Emily Demuth

CRISPIN BOOKS

Crispin Books is an independent press based in Milwaukee, Wisconsin. With its sibling imprint, Crickhollow Books, Crispin publishes quality fiction and nonfiction for discerning readers.

For a complete list of books in print, visit:

www.CrispinBooks.com

or

www.CrickhollowBooks.com

Hattie's War
© 2014, Hilda and Emily Demuth

This is a work of fiction. Although some episodes and a few characters in the story are loosely based on historical events and persons, as noted in the acknowledgements at the end of the book, the characters are primarily drawn from the authors' imaginations.

Cover design by Kyle Smart
Cover photo by Gretchen Demuth Hansen

Original Trade Softcover
ISBN: 978-1-883953-76-8

In memory
of
Jane V. Lynch

and
the gallant ladies
of the
West Side Soldiers' Aid Society

April 1864

1.

AT THE CRACK OF TEDDY'S BAT, Hattie Bigelow squinted into the sunlight. Starched petticoats swishing, she scurried across the big lawn in the direction of the base ball arcing toward her through the sky. The ball bounced once on the grass before the eleven-year-old girl caught it, the tough leather stinging her hands. She raised it triumphantly. Above the Bigelows' three-story house, a seagull that had strayed from the nearby Milwaukee River added its squawks to the applause of the onlookers on the wide back porch.

"You're out, Teddy," called Mr. Jenkins, the pitcher. "Nice work, Hattie."

Hattie's younger brother Teddy scowled and dropped the bat in disgust.

Hattie grinned as she tossed the ball back to Mr. Jenkins.

"My turn," said Charlie Moores, stepping forward from his catcher's position at the edge of the garden.

The Bigelows' next-door neighbor Charlie was four years older than Hattie. With a confident smile and a quick wave to the onlookers, he took his stance at home plate, his curly dark hair glistening in the sunlight as he gave the bat a couple of practice swings.

"We'd best move back!" Hattie called to Teddy's classmate George Schaefer, as she retreated as fast as she could in her stiff petticoats. She positioned herself near the lilacs that bordered her family's yard, the favorite neighborhood gathering place.

Mr. Jenkins' steady underhand pitch sailed toward Charlie, whose full swing sent the ball flying clean out of the Bigelow yard and over the corner of the next-door Moores yard to land with a thud near the Schaefer outhouse.

Charlie's little sisters, Molly and Bea, jumped up from their perch on the porch steps, shrieking and applauding as Charlie rounded the bases, while George scrambled through the lilac hedge to fetch the ball.

"Well struck!" said Mr. Jenkins. "Charlie Moores, when the Milwaukee Base Ball Club starts up again, I hope to see you on my side."

Huffing and puffing, George appeared a few moments later from the lilacs and tossed the ball to Mr. Jenkins, who looked around and said, "Who's the next striker?"

"It's my turn!" Hattie loped across the yard, her petticoats bobbing, and picked up the bat.

Teddy snorted. "You can't hit a ball."

Hattie glared at her brother.

George caught his breath, his thin face red under his blonde hair. "It's my turn to strike. Besides, girls don't play real base ball anyway. Right, Charlie?"

Charlie shrugged. "I believe base ball is a *gentleman's* game. Isn't that so, Mister Jenkins?"

Those words stung Hattie more than the ball had. "Didn't I catch the ball?" She brandished the bat in George's direction, and let her challenge hang in the air. George had no answer, and she saw Charlie smile.

All of the children looked at Mr. Jenkins, who said, "Take your stance, Hattie."

As the ball sailed toward her, Hattie swung the bat ferociously, determined to show the boys a mighty hit. She missed and whirled sideways, the force of her swing tangling the bat in her petticoats.

The boys snickered, and the little girls giggled.

"You're not chopping a tree, Hattie," said Mr. Jenkins. "Swing straight—just meet the ball and let the bat do the work."

Hattie took a deep breath and nodded. She waited for the next pitch. As she swung straight and sure, the bat connected with the leather ball and sent it bouncing briskly across the yard.

"Run, Hattie!" called Molly and Bea.

The little girls squealed and clapped their hands as Hattie pounded across the yard, arms churning and sturdy black boots flying. She arrived safely on first base before Teddy retrieved the ball and lobbed it to Mr. Jenkins.

Hattie folded her arms across her chest and glared at George. "I told you I could hit."

The back door creaked as Mother stepped out onto the porch. "Mister Jenkins, Ellen is ready to serve your tea." She looked at Hattie. "Whatever have you been doing?

Your face is all red, and your pinafore is askew."

Mr. Jenkins waved the players in from the yard, rolling down his white shirt sleeves and picking up his jacket from the porch rail on his way into the house.

"I never even got to strike," muttered George. His shoulders slumped, but then he straightened up. "I'd best get home. Ma says I'm the man of the family till Pa gets back from the war."

"Come along, girls," said Charlie. Molly and Bea hopped off the porch and followed him through the break in the hedge. Hattie waved at Charlie and called out, "Let's play again soon!"

Stepping gracefully down from the porch, her hoops swaying, Mother surveyed the yard like a commanding officer. "Teddy, fetch the croquet hoops from the garden shed."

Teddy blinked. "Are we going to play croquet after tea?"

"I've no time for such things. One of the men from St. Gall's is coming to break ground for a bigger garden. We need to mark out the area for him."

Hattie frowned. "Why do we need a bigger garden?"

Mother sighed. "Hattie, I'm sure I have explained that all of us on the West Side are to plant more vegetables to supply the new Soldiers' Home."

Teddy trotted up with the wire hoops slung over his arm. Mother walked slowly across the lawn, directing her son to stick a hoop into the grass every several yards.

Hattie stared in disbelief. The new garden plot would swallow up most of the yard. "There's no place left for us to play!" She followed after Teddy and began to pull up the hoops.

"Hattie Bigelow, whatever are you doing?"

"This is home plate," Hattie said, pointing toward the burlap bag on the lawn. "You can't put a garden here!"

"Feeding hungry soldiers is more important than playing ball. All of us must do our part to support the cause. Don't you want to preserve the Union?"

Hattie scowled. "Oh, Mother. The war's been going on for *years*. We never needed such a big garden before."

"Do you know how many soldiers come through Milwaukee every week?" Mother's voice was tight. "You and Teddy *will* take charge of the garden this summer."

Hattie snatched up another hoop. "If we're taking charge," she snapped, "why can't we put the garden wherever we want?"

"Hattie Bigelow!" boomed a voice from the street. "You are *never* to speak to your mother that way."

Father stood at the garden gate, his mouth stern beneath his gray whiskers.

Hattie stared sullenly at the croquet hoops on the grass.

Teddy promptly started replacing the wire hoops. Slowly Hattie stooped to help him.

Father watched them in silence for a moment before he pushed open the gate to enter the yard.

Tears stung Hattie's eyes. But Teddy did as his mother commanded, forming a front line of hoops, like little soldiers, marching right through the middle of the yard.

2.

H ATTIE GALLOPED DOWN THE STEPS the next morning, skidding to a halt in the doorway of the dining room. She was late again. All of the other members of the household—Father, Mother, Teddy, Mr. Jenkins, who was renting a room, and Miss Taft, the other boarder—were already seated at the table. Hattie slipped into the chair beside Teddy under Mother's reproachful gaze.

Ellen, the housekeeper, swung open the door from the kitchen and set a platter of ham and potatoes in front of Father. "'Tis a fair morning," she said, bustling around the table with the toast rack and dishes of jelly.

"Thank you, Ellen," said Mother. "Hattie, after breakfast you are to help me collect more supplies for the Soldiers' Home."

"Can't that wait? Teddy and I need to play ball in the yard one last time before it's ruined."

"No, the Soldiers' Home cannot wait. Half of the beds are already filled, and more men arrive every day. We need supplies now."

"How many beds do you have in all?" asked Mr. Jenkins as he helped himself to a slice of ham.

"Twenty so far on the main floor. We separated the sleeping quarters from a sitting room. Missus Buttrick insists that the soldiers have pleasant surroundings that remind them of home."

"Why do the soldiers need a special home?" asked Teddy. "Why don't the sick ones go back to live with their families?"

Miss Taft set down her tea cup. "Many of the Wisconsin soldiers are immigrants," she said. "Some of them have no relatives in this country to look after them."

Hattie wished Teddy had not asked a question that made Miss Taft sound as if she were standing in her classroom at the Fourth Ward School.

Mother passed the potatoes. "The mission of the Home is to look after our boys—until they are able to support themselves or return to their families."

Father looked up from his plate and shook his head. "That is an admirable goal. But those who are badly maimed will never work again. You ladies can't care for them forever in your pretty rented rooms."

Mother's butter knife scraped sharply across her toast.

"But it's a noble effort, to be sure," said Mr. Jenkins.

After breakfast Father left for his boot and shoe shop and Mr. Jenkins for his law office in City Hall. Miss Taft returned to her room upstairs to correct papers.

Teddy scampered outside to play while Hattie cleared the table and carried the dishes to the kitchen.

"Set them right here, there's a dear," said Ellen as she poured hot water into the sink.

Hattie glanced out the kitchen window. "There's a man at the gate."

"That would be Jerry, from St. Gall's. Let him in, then."

The jolly-faced man outside the gate tipped his cap to her. "Top o' the morning!" he called. "I've come to do some diggin' for ye." He trundled a wheelbarrow through the gate, a shovel clanging against the post as he entered the yard. Nodding at the lines of croquet hoops, he said, "I see ye've marked it out for me. Fine work, that."

Silently Hattie walked across her base ball field one last time, her steps heavy, and stood in the middle of the yard.

"Hattie!" Mother called from an upstairs window. "Come and help!"

Reluctantly Hattie climbed the stairs to the second floor, where Mother was pulling bed sheets from the linen closet in the hallway. "We'll sort through all of the sheets and blankets and decide which to donate to the Soldiers' Home."

By the time Hattie carried a stack of folded sheets and wool blankets down to the back porch, Jerry had dug a trench alongside the line of croquet hoops, cutting off home plate from the base ball diamond by a long black gash.

May 1864

3.

ONE AFTERNOON when Hattie and Teddy came home from playing in George's yard, Mother met them at the back door and pointed to a bulging burlap sack on the porch. "Ask Ellen the best way to plant these seed potatoes. I'm off to meet Missus Buttrick about donations for the Soldiers' Home." With a rustle of silk she made her way carefully along the narrow strip of grass to the gate.

Hattie slumped against the porch rail. She preferred burlap sacks sewn into square bases stuffed with sawdust.

Teddy dropped his books and stooped to pull out a dirt-crusted potato. "Do you reckon we just bury 'em in the ground?" Holding the potato, he trotted into the house, and the door banged shut behind him.

Hattie picked up his books and followed him inside.

In the kitchen Teddy set the potato on the tray beside a teacake.

"Teddy Bigelow, are you thinking Miss Taft wants a dirty potato with her tea? Out with you now!"

Teddy picked up the potato, and Ellen whisked away

the cloth to replace it with another.

"But we need to know how to plant these."

Ellen pointed to a tiny green bud on the skin. "That's an eye. When you cut up potatoes for planting, every piece must have an eye."

"Why is that?" asked Hattie.

"So it can see to grow, of course."

The back door creaked, and Ellen sang out, "Good afternoon to you, Miss Taft! I'll be servin' tea directly." She turned to Hattie. "Put on a pleasant face now and go into the parlor. Teddy, mind you leave that potato here."

In the parlor Miss Taft peered down her sharp nose and said, "Good afternoon, children. How do you intend to spend this beautiful afternoon?"

Teddy responded cheerfully, "We're going to plant potatoes, ma'am."

Ellen entered with the tray. "Oh, but never today, Teddy! You can't be planting potatoes till next week—or two weeks ago. Not till the dark of the moon."

Hattie wrinkled her brow. "Why would we plant at night?"

"Ellen doesn't mean the dark of night," said Miss Taft. "The 'dark of the moon' is the darkening—or waning—from the full moon to the new." As Ellen poured tea from the china pot, Miss Taft continued, "You see, children, some people believe that crops should be planted according to the phase of the moon. This is mere folklore, of course."

Ellen tilted her head. "Beggin' your pardon, but some people do know a thing or two about gardening. Back in

Ireland the Carrolls were the finest of gardeners."

Miss Taft stirred cream into her tea. "Children, you can plant those potatoes whenever you please, and it won't make a speck of difference."

Rather gruffly, Ellen said, "Enjoy your tea, Miss Taft," and left the parlor.

When clanking and clattering erupted from the kitchen, Miss Taft raised her eyebrows and sipped her tea. "I hope you will use modern methods to plant your garden."

"Yes, ma'am." Hattie nudged Teddy and together they sidled to the doorway.

Once they were safely outside, Teddy said, "Do you think we ought to plant the potatoes today?"

Hattie sank onto the porch step and rested her chin in her hands. "Mother won't be pleased if we don't."

Teddy plopped down beside her. "And she won't be pleased if the potatoes don't grow."

"Oh, Teddy, of course they'll grow."

"But Ellen said—"

"Ellen is a housekeeper. Miss Taft is a *teacher*."

Teddy frowned. "You needn't talk as if Miss Taft is better than Ellen."

"I didn't mean that. I only meant—"

A piercing whistle from the street interrupted them, and Charlie Moores leaned over the gate. "Hattie and Teddy, have you heard the news? I'm going to do my part for the Union—I've signed up!"

After a moment of shocked silence, Teddy leaped to his feet and punched his fist into the air. "Huzzah! Three cheers for Charlie!"

Hattie blinked. "But you're just fifteen. How can you be a soldier?"

Charlie's brow furrowed. "Hattie, I'm almost sixteen. I've signed up as a musician. A drummer. Next month I'll be drumming the orders for Colonel Buttrick in the Thirty-ninth Wisconsin Infantry."

Hattie felt a clutch at her heart. "How—how long will you be gone?"

"President Lincoln has called for new regiments to serve just a hundred days. It seems he needs us Hundred Days men to guard Union territory so other troops can move deeper South. Don't worry about me, Hattie. In three months we'll lick those Rebels and the war will be over."

Ten-year-old Teddy stared wistfully at the older boy. "I hope the war lasts long enough for me to sign up."

Charlie grinned. "I don't know about that, Teddy. Besides, I'm not sure your father can spare me that long from his shop."

"Have you told Father you're leaving?" Hattie asked.

"Yes, I did before I enlisted. I wanted to be sure he would hold my place until I return."

"Perhaps I could sell boots and shoes this summer," said Hattie.

The boys exchanged knowing glances. Then Charlie said, "Hattie, even I spend most of my time sweeping floors and polishing boots, not selling brogans. Besides, you're a girl."

Teddy nodded. "Nobody would want to buy boots and shoes from a lady. Perhaps Father will ask me to help."

Hattie glared at them. "That isn't fair. And Charlie, you needn't talk as if you're better than I am."

Charlie stopped smiling. "No, it's not that. I only meant that men and women are . . . well, different. Everybody knows that." He stepped back from the gate. "I'm off to spread the good news."

Hattie watched her neighbor stride away down the wooden sidewalk. She looked down at the ground, then across the yard with its long trench.

With no base ball and no Charlie, the next hundred days would be miserable indeed.

4.

WHEN HATTIE AND TEDDY arrived home from school the following afternoon, they stood in the back yard eyeing the long rows staked by broken pickets.

"According to the Old Farmers' Almanac, the moon will be full in two weeks," said Hattie. "When we plant the rest of the potatoes, we'll carve a little moon on each picket to mark them as Ellen's rows."

"Miss Taft's rows will have sprouted by then," said Teddy.

Hattie nodded. "But dividing the planting in half was the fair thing to do."

In the kitchen Hattie heard the gabble of women's voices from the parlor. Today Mother was hosting the Soldiers' Home Society meeting.

Ellen allowed Hattie and Teddy to take one teacake each from the silver tray.

Teddy licked his sticky fingers. "I'd rather not go in to see the ladies. They fuss too much. I'm going to play catch in George's yard."

Ellen smiled. "Off with you, boyo."

As Hattie turned to follow him, Ellen said, "Whist now, darlin'. I need you to help me serve the tea."

Hattie sighed. "Yes, Ellen."

The back door banged shut behind Teddy.

Hattie followed the housekeeper down the hall, the tea cart rolling with a faint clinking of china. Just outside the parlor, Ellen whispered, "Mind you now, we mustn't go in till Missus Hewitt declares the meeting is adjourned."

"What does 'adjourned' mean?"

"Means 'tis time to talk about something more interesting."

Hattie peeked into the parlor. All of the members of the Soldiers' Home Society except the president and the secretary had needlework in their hands. Mother seemed more intent on stitching a carpet slipper than on listening to the report of numbers of soldiers in residence and the amount of meat purchased.

Mrs. Buttrick looked up from the sock she was knitting. She smiled at Hattie, who stood in the doorway.

Hattie liked Mrs. Buttrick best of all the ladies. She was younger than Mother and never sharp or cross.

Mrs. Hewitt, the president, reminded everyone to record all donations to the Home and submit a monthly report to the newspaper. Then she turned to Mrs. Buttrick. "Now, I believe our vice-president has an important announcement to make."

Mrs. Buttrick laid down her knitting. "As you know, Colonel Buttrick has been appointed commander of the Thirty-ninth. All of the Hundred Days regiments will depart in June. I am thrilled to tell you that the colonel and I have decided that I ought to accompany the Thirty-ninth on this important assignment."

A burst of excitement followed this proclamation as the other women bombarded the colonel's wife with questions.

Mrs. Hewitt called for silence, then asked Mrs. Vedder, who sat at the writing desk in the corner, "Is there any other business?"

The secretary shook her head.

"The meeting is adjourned."

At Ellen's nod, Hattie rolled the tea cart into the parlor. Most of the members of the Society set aside their needlework, but Mrs. Eisenmenger held up a beaded drawstring bag for a neighbor to admire. "It's for my Lizzie. She wants one just like mine. How could a mother resist?"

Mother poured tea into a cup, placed a spoon on the saucer, and murmured, "Take the first to Missus Hewitt. And the second to Missus Buttrick."

When Hattie delivered the vice-president her tea, Mrs. Buttrick thanked her and added, "Hattie, I told Mister Jenkins our local base ball players ought to get up a kind of send-off before the regiment departs. I hope to see you out at Camp Scott cheering on your side."

"Yes, ma'am!" Hattie smiled to herself as she continued to carry cups of tea to the ladies.

"My goodness, Hattie Bigelow," said Mrs. Eisenmenger as Hattie approached her chair. "What a big girl you are! My Lizzie is just a little thing with such dainty hands and feet. I suppose your father can hardly keep you in shoes."

Hattie glanced down to inspect the boot sticking out from below her skirts. The saucer tilted, the tea sloshed, and the cup and spoon slid right onto Mrs. Eisenmenger's lap.

Mrs. Eisenmenger lurched from her chair, and the cup thumped onto the carpet, the spoon jangling after it.

"Clumsy girl!" she sputtered, holding the dripping bead-work well away from the dark stain on her skirt.

Cheeks burning, Hattie knelt to pick up the cup and spoon, stammering, "I'm so sorry. I didn't mean to—"

"Ellen, come here at once!" Mother called.

Hattie straightened up with the cup in one hand and the saucer in the other. "I was only trying to help," she said. "I'm truly sorry—"

Hattie fled the parlor and stumbled out the back door, down the porch steps, and across the yard, pushing deep into the fragrant lilac bushes. She sat with her back against the trunk of the oldest bush, drawing her knees up within the circle of her arms. For a few moments all she could hear was her own panting breath and the echo of Mrs. Eisenmenger's hateful words.

The nearby branches rustled, and Teddy peered out from among the heart-shaped leaves, holding a base ball. "What's wrong, Hattie?"

"Nothing. Go away."

He nodded wisely. "I *told* you those ladies fuss too much."

5.

A FTER SCHOOL the next day Hattie walked straight to the parlor without even setting down her books. Teddy scurried after her, following so closely that he almost bumped into her when she halted to inspect the floor beside the table.

"What are you looking at?" he asked.

Hattie satisfied herself that there was no tea stain on the floral carpet. "Nothing."

Teddy poked at the rounded cutout pieces of carpet on the table and sighed. "Mother's hardly ever home anymore."

"It's her week to supervise the Soldiers' Home." Hattie tried not to think of Mother's angry face at yesterday's meeting. She walked to the writing desk where Mrs. Vedder had sat. A sheet of paper lay on the slanted oak top. Hattie read the list of requested items and said slowly, "The Soldiers' Home needs a writing desk. Wouldn't Mother be pleased if we delivered this one?"

She lifted the hinged lid and peered inside while Teddy measured the width of the desk with his hands. "I'll get my wagon and bring it 'round to the front." He trotted out of the parlor.

Hattie pulled out sheets of letterhead stationery with

the words "Bigelow & Co." below a drawing of an elephant wearing boots and waving a flag. She took out bundles of letters and the marbled ledger in which Mother kept household accounts, setting them on the stack of *Harper's* magazines in the bookcase.

Teddy returned to the parlor with a length of cord. "We'd best batten down the hatches before we set sail."

Hattie watched her brother wrap the cord deftly over and under the desk, binding the lid securely to the frame. Nobody would ever call Teddy clumsy.

She and Teddy carefully maneuvered the desk out onto the front porch and down the steps. They set the desk upside down on top of the wooden wagon.

Hattie eyed the four desk legs sticking up in the air like masts on a ship as Teddy knotted the cord to fasten the desk securely. She took off her pinafore and tied it across two of the legs.

Teddy grinned. "Hoist that sail, matey!"

They headed east on Clybourn Street toward the river, Teddy pulling and Hattie pushing the load over the sidewalk.

At each street crossing, Hattie had to hold the desk steady as the wagon bumped down into the roadway and up again onto the sidewalk on the other side. After several blocks Teddy sang out, "Hard portside, matey!" and they turned north onto Second Street.

"*My Bonnie lies over the ocean,*" he sang in time to the thumping of the wheels, "*My Bonnie lies over the sea . . .*"

Hattie joined in on the refrain: "*Oh, bring back my Bonnie to me!*"

As the wagon passed St. Gall's Church and the construction site for the new Catholic school, several workmen added their deep voices to the refrain. When the song ended, other workers whistled and clapped their hands.

Teddy chose to turn east again for a block and then swing north onto West Water Street with its long line of tall storefronts and warehouses along the west bank of the Milwaukee River. White gulls swooped and squabbled overhead, and perspiration beaded on Hattie's forehead. She wished she had thought to put on a hat. She began to sing again, making her voice boom out like those of the workmen at St. Gall's. *"Way, haul away, we'll haul away togeh-heh-ther! Way, haul away, haul away, Joe!"*

Teddy made his voice deep, too, and together they growled out the sea shanty as if they were indeed aboard a ship—*"Way, haul away, haul away, Joe!"*

Outside Birchard's Hall stood Mrs. Eisenmenger with her daughter Lizzie. Blinking away the sweat stinging her eyes, Hattie noted miserably that the pink gloves holding Lizzie's parasol exactly matched the ribbons on her hat.

"Good afternoon, Missus Eisenmenger," said Teddy cheerfully. "We're bound for the Soldiers' Home."

Mrs. Eisenmenger smiled at Teddy. "Is that so?" She did not smile at Hattie, who had never felt bigger or clumsier in her life.

"Yes, ma'am," said Teddy, "and we'd best be off again while we have a fair wind." He yanked the handle of the wagon. *"Way, haul away, we'll haul away togeh-heh-ther—"*

Hattie grabbed the desk legs as the wagon lurched forward. Out of the corner of her eye she saw Lizzie whisper to her mother behind one dainty pink glove. For the rest of the voyage to the Soldiers' Home, Teddy was the only one who sang.

6.

T HEY HALTED IN FRONT of the building rented by the Soldiers' Home Society, a tall cream-colored brick storefront that had previously been the site of first-floor shops and second-floor offices. Hattie saw new curtains hanging in the wide front windows.

Teddy turned to Hattie. "Should we go 'round to the back?" he asked. "This is a delivery, after all."

The children trundled the wagon down the narrow alley between the neighboring building and the Soldiers' Home. The unpainted porch at the back door was piled with empty crates, bushel baskets, and barrels from soldiers' aid societies all over Wisconsin.

Hattie stepped up to the door and rapped sharply. The door opened and Mother appeared, clearly startled.

"Hattie, what are you doing here?" Mother stared at the wagon. "And what in the name of goodness is that?"

"We've come to make a donation."

"Hattie Bigelow, whatever do you mean, removing that desk from our parlor? You take that wagon home directly."

Hattie gaped at her. "But the Soldiers' Home needs a writing desk. I saw the list from the meeting."

"That is the *Bigelow* desk. It was built by your great-grandfather back in Massachusetts. You are to take that wagon home." Mother stepped back inside and shut the door.

This time her mother's anger struck sparks in Hattie. As they stood outside, she looked at Teddy and shook her head.

"She's forever telling us we need to make sacrifices to help the soldiers. If this is the Bigelow desk, Teddy, we'll go talk to Father about it."

Leaving the wagon and desk in the alley, Hattie and Teddy marched across the bridge to East Water Street, which ran parallel to West Water Street on the opposite side of the river. After passing several brick storefronts, Hattie saw the elephant signboard of Bigelow & Company.

She flung open the door, setting the tin bell jangling. Charlie Moores glanced up from behind a display of soldiers' brogans, but Hattie marched straight up to the counter where Father stood talking with a uniformed soldier. "Pardon me," she said politely, "but I must speak to my father."

Father raised his eyebrows. "This is a place of business, Hattie girl. You will sit over there and wait your turn." He turned back to the soldier. "I apologize for my daughter, Sergeant."

Her cheeks burning, Hattie sat on the customers' bench.

Teddy plopped down beside her, inhaling the smells of leather and neatsfoot oil. "I'm going to like working here."

"Oh, hush, Teddy! Father hasn't even asked you."

At the counter the soldier signed a paper, shook hands with Father, and left the shop, the tin bell jangling behind him. Then Father fixed his daughter with a stern look.

"I'm sorry I spoke out of turn," Hattie said, "but the Soldiers' Home needs a desk. So we took that old one from the parlor."

Father raised his eyebrows again. "The Bigelow desk? That was my father's desk—and his father's before him. That desk always belongs to the oldest son."

Teddy beamed. "Then it's *my* desk! And I choose to lend it to the Soldiers' Home." He slid off the bench. "Hattie, we'd best go tell Mother. Good afternoon, Father!" he called as he trotted toward the door.

Hattie avoided her father's eyes as she followed Teddy out of the shop.

Teddy skipped cheerfully ahead as they crossed the bridge and turned down West Water Street, but when they rounded the corner of the Soldiers' Home, the little wagon beside the unpainted porch was empty.

The back door creaked open, and Mother stepped out so quickly that her narrow hoops bounced against the doorframe.

"Where's my Bigelow desk?" Teddy asked. "I've decided to let the soldiers use it until I need it."

Mother hurried down the porch steps and stooped to embrace him. "My dear boy, how very kind you are."

Teddy wriggled uncomfortably in her grasp. "What happened to the desk?"

Mother smiled, her eyes glistening. "Come in and see."

Hattie exchanged glances with her brother as they followed Mother into the Soldiers' Home. Just inside the back door hung a row of blue uniform coats and kepis. Narrow beds with scarlet coverlets filled the main room, and tall folding screens separated the sleeping quarters from the upholstered furniture and reading lamps and bookcase in the sitting room. Near the curtained front window a thin young soldier sat at the desk, his gaze intent upon the pen moving slowly over the page, as he carefully composed a letter. A pair of crutches leaned alongside his chair.

Mother ignored Hattie as she leaned down to kiss the top of Teddy's head. "You sweet, generous boy."

June 1864

7.

THE BRIM OF HATTIE'S SUNBONNET blocked out the world beyond the garden. She moved slowly along the rows, stooping to pluck out every single weed without disturbing the soil around each tiny plant. With a grunt she straightened up to stretch her aching back and wipe the sweat from her forehead.

At each end of the long green lines fringing the dark soil, broken pickets marked the rows of onions and carrots and beans and turnips and potatoes. It seemed unlikely that the delicate sets of leaves, barely visible in Ellen's rows, would ever catch up to the potato plants in Miss Taft's rows.

Teddy worked steadily in the next row, mumbling threats to an invisible enemy. "You won't escape me, you dirty Reb. I see you hiding. Surrender at once!"

"Hullo, Teddy!" came the familiar call as George Schaefer trotted into the yard and stood at the edge of the garden, tossing a base ball from hand to hand. "Let's play catch in my yard."

Instantly Teddy straightened up and brushed the dirt from his knees.

Hattie frowned. "Teddy Bigelow, don't even think of leaving before you've finished your work. It's not fair to leave it to me."

Teddy grinned. "You sound like Mother—or Miss Taft."

A peal of laughter sounded from the sidewalk. "She surely does!"

Hattie turned to see her classmate Lizzie Eisenmenger standing outside the gate, holding her parasol carefully to shade her eyes from the sun.

"What are you doing here?" Hattie impatiently brushed the dirt off her work dress.

Lizzie smirked. "I don't see that it's any concern of yours if I stroll down the sidewalk."

Hattie shrugged and turned away just in time to see Teddy and George disappearing through the lilac hedge. She was about to call after them but thought better of it. She kicked a clod of dirt and bent back to her task, glad now that the sunbonnet's brim blocked out the world beyond the garden.

"Still," said Lizzie loudly, "since you ask, I'll tell you that I've formed the Fourth Ward School Girls' Sewing Society. We're meeting at Mary Ann's this afternoon—" Lizzie sighed. "Though I'm not sure you'll be presentable enough to attend."

Hattie gritted her teeth and did not respond, but she heard the shrill voices of the Moores girls calling "Lizzie! It's Lizzie Eisenmenger!" as they charged out from the house next door. Hattie devoted herself to plucking weeds from the row of fernlike carrot tops, but she could not help but hear the conversation over the fence.

Molly cooed, "I *love* your parasol!"

"So do I," breathed Bea.

"My goodness, you girls are sweet to say so. Where's your brother Charlie?"

"He's working at Mister Bigelow's shop," said Molly.

Lizzie sighed again. "We'll certainly miss our Charlie when he's gone to war, won't we? Did your mama cry when he told her he'd signed up?"

Hattie crushed a handful of weeds in her fist.

"Mama said they were tears of joy," Molly reported. "She said we must be very proud of him."

"Why, of course we must. Still, it's dreadful to think of his being in danger, isn't it?"

"But he's a drummer," Bea said slowly. "Mama said the Rebs don't aim at musicians."

Hattie flung down the weeds and straightened up, pushing back her sunbonnet. "That's right," she said, glaring over the fence at the face shaded by the parasol. "Isn't that so, Lizzie?"

Lizzie stepped away from the gate. "I didn't know you were such an expert on the war, Hattie Bigelow." She twirled her parasol a few more times. "I'd best get to my meeting. Today we're sewing bags for coffee and sugar and salt. Perhaps Charlie will get the ones that I make."

She smiled at the Moores girls and sauntered away.

Hattie watched the parasol grow smaller in the distance, as she heard Molly say, "She's so pretty."

Bea chimed in. "I hope Charlie gets the bags she makes."

Hattie wiped her dirty hands down her pinafore, leaving long dark smears. "Girls, do you think you could find Teddy, please? Tell him he'd best finish his rows before Ellen calls us in to supper."

8.

ON A BRIGHT AFTERNOON Hattie snatched her straw hat from the peg and hurried to the back door. Today the Milwaukee Base Ball Club was getting up a game for the Hundred Days regiments. When she shoved the door open, she nearly ran into Miss Taft on the porch.

"I beg your pardon, ma'am," she said promptly, hastily tying the ribbons under her chin.

Miss Taft merely continued her conversation with Teddy and George, who stood side by side at the bottom of the steps. "You boys have a good time at the game."

"Yes, ma'am!" they chorused before they raced each other to the gate and grappled for the privilege of passing through first.

Hattie tried to sidle past Miss Taft, but the teacher turned to her with a smile. "Hattie, I was just thinking of you. I met Missus Eisenmenger in town, and she told me that Lizzie's sewing circle has been working valiantly on the soldiers' bags. I told her every girl in the Fourth Ward would be glad to help. The girls are gathering at Lizzie's house now. Wouldn't you like to join them?"

Hattie's heart sank. "Now?" She shook her head. "I can't, ma'am. I'm going to the game."

"Sometimes we must put others' needs before our own pleasures. Your classmates have been working very hard.

Think how disappointed they will be if they don't reach their goal."

"I'm sorry, Miss Taft, I truly am, but I can't sew today." Hattie looked around desperately for a way to escape.

"Hattie Bigelow, I'm surprised at you. I should think you'd want to do your part to help the soldiers."

"Do my part? Don't you see me working every day in that horrid garden till I'm filthy and sweating?" Hattie felt as if she would explode. "Besides, Lizzie doesn't want me at her old sewing circle anyway." Abruptly she scrambled over the porch rail and dropped into the flower bed, dashed out through the gate, and galloped down the sidewalk after Teddy and George.

Why hadn't the boys waited for her? And why didn't Miss Taft ever ask *them* to sacrifice their pleasures for others' needs?

Hattie hurried block after block toward the fairgrounds, passing wagons and buggies until she was completely out of breath. A matched pair of horses pulling a fine carriage trotted swiftly past her.

"Driver, please halt!"

The commanding voice was familiar, and Hattie turned to see Mrs. Buttrick smiling at her.

"Good afternoon, Hattie. Would you like a ride?"

Gratefully Hattie climbed into the carriage. Mrs. Buttrick smoothed her hoops to make room for Hattie and introduced her to two pale, thin soldiers in the opposite seat. "Private Bauer and Private Mackenzie come from farms near Oshkosh. They've never seen a base ball game."

Hattie smiled at the soldiers. "I hope you enjoy the

game." She tried not to stare at the empty sleeve pinned neatly to Private Mackenzie's blue uniform. He seemed to be only a few years older than Charlie.

When the carriage halted at the entrance to the fairgrounds, now known as Camp Scott, Mrs. Buttrick leaned out to say a few cheerful words to the young soldier standing guard. Camp Scott consisted of officers' barracks and a dining hall and a city of tents. The parade grounds for marching and drilling was the same field, Hattie knew, where Mr. Jenkins and his new base ball club had played their first games only a year before the war began.

The driver helped Mrs. Buttrick out of the carriage and stood close by as the two soldiers stepped down. When the driver pulled three wooden folding chairs from the back of the carriage, Private Bauer said gruffly, "I'll take those."

Mrs. Buttrick said, "Hattie, would you please carry the quilt for me?" Turning to the young soldier, she said, "Private Mackenzie, would you mind escorting me to that tree?"

The soldier smiled, and Mrs. Buttrick slipped her arm through the crook of his good elbow.

Most of the other spectators had gathered in the shade of an enormous oak. Private Bauer set the chairs in a row, and Hattie spread the quilt near Mrs. Buttrick's chair.

"Thank you, Hattie. Now run along to your friends. I see your brother over there."

Hattie trotted over to Teddy and George, who stood beside Charlie Moores.

Charlie greeted Hattie, but Teddy and George kept watching Mr. Jenkins and the other team captain nearby.

The other players milled about, eager to begin the game.

"Best get your last licks in today," called one of the men to another. "You won't be seeing much play down in Memphis."

"You never know," said the other. "I reckon the Thirty-ninth can scare the Rebs so far away we'll have plenty of time to toss a ball around."

Mr. Jenkins looked down the two rows of players. "We're a man short," he said. Turning to Hattie and her companions, he called, "Charlie, come and fill in, will you?"

Charlie grinned as he joined the older men. He stood proudly among the lawyers and shopkeepers and city officials who had left their workplaces on this perfect summer day to enjoy the novelty of the pastime known as base ball.

Teddy and George clapped their hands and whistled. "Go, Charlie! Show 'em what you're made of!"

The Gent, the club member who would monitor the game, shooed the children back to the shade of the oak tree. Hattie sank down onto the quilt. The Gent approached the spectators and said, "Ladies, it's quite warm in the sun, and the players have asked whether they might roll up their sleeves."

Mrs. Buttrick glanced at the other women present, and together they gave their consent.

The Gent nodded to the players, who hastily undid their cuffs and rolled up their sleeves as they took their positions on the field.

"Do you think the Hundred Days men will get to play base ball?" Hattie asked Mrs. Buttrick.

Mrs. Buttrick smiled under the wide brim of her hat.

"I don't know, Hattie. The days down in Memphis will be dreadfully hot. But if our boys do play, I'll be there to cheer them on."

Hattie turned back to the field to see Mr. Jenkins standing beside home plate, as the game began. His solid hit on the first pitch sent the ball far afield.

"Huzzah!" sang out Mrs. Buttrick.

"Well struck!" Hattie called.

9.

W HEN THE DAY ARRIVED for the Hundred Days
regiments to depart, Hattie and Teddy dutifully
weeded their rows until Ellen called from the back porch,
"Children! Have you forgotten the time? You don't want to
miss the grand send-off!"

Teddy nearly smashed the cucumber plants in his
haste as he scrambled across the rows. "Hurry, Hattie, or
we won't get to see Charlie!"

Hattie sloshed her hands in a pail of water and dried
them on her soiled pinafore. She pulled off her sunbonnet
and untied her pinafore as Ellen held out her straw hat.

The housekeeper smoothed Hattie's straight brown
hair and tied the ribbon under her chin. "You must be sure
to send my love to young Charlie and tell him all of St.
Gall's Church will be praying for his safe return. And you
must take a remembrance. 'Tis bad luck to say farewell
empty-handed."

Hattie glanced at the white roses spilling over the trel-
lis beside the porch. "Teddy, give me your knife."

Teddy pulled a penknife from his pocket and cut a cluster of white roses himself. "Ouch," he said as he thrust the
flowers at Hattie. "There. Now *please* let's go."

Gingerly holding the roses, Hattie scurried through the
gate and down the sidewalk after Teddy.

Long before she arrived at the square, Hattie could hear a brass band playing a rousing version of "The Girl I Left Behind Me." City Hall was festooned with red, white, and blue bunting. Women wept and embraced husbands and sons, and scores of children gaped at the vast expanse of blue uniforms where the regiment gathered.

Teddy grabbed Hattie's free hand and began to snake through the forest of blue trousers. Hattie said "Pardon me" and "I beg your pardon" over and over as her skirts brushed against muskets and haversacks, and could not help but tread on the toes of leather brogans as she squirmed through the crowd.

"I see Colonel Buttrick on the steps," Teddy said. "The drummers must be nearby."

Hattie stood on tiptoe to glimpse the commanding officer of the Thirty-ninth Wisconsin regiment, impressive in his gold-braided uniform, sword at his side. Mrs. Buttrick stood beside him in a dark traveling cloak, a tri-color rosette pinned to her collar.

Hattie turned to Teddy. "We ought to speak to Missus Buttrick."

"We needn't talk to the ladies—only the soldiers."

Hattie gripped Teddy's hand tighter and pulled him toward the Buttricks. "She's going to war, the same as any man or boy."

Teddy snorted. "She's not carrying a rifle or even a drum." But he nodded politely when he and Hattie stood before the colonel and his wife.

"Good afternoon, Missus Buttrick," Hattie said. "We

hope you have a pleasant journey."

Mrs. Buttrick smiled. "Thank you, Hattie. I'm sure this will be an adventure, though some parts may be far from pleasant."

"Will you sleep in a tent?" Teddy asked.

"I hope not. In Memphis I expect we'll find a building to serve as an infirmary. I intend to nurse any of our boys who take ill."

Hattie nodded. "Just the way you do at the Soldiers' Home."

"Exactly. And I'm counting on you children to continue doing your part here in Milwaukee."

"There's Charlie!" said Teddy abruptly, turning to push his way through the throng to the regimental musicians.

Hattie blushed at Teddy's rudeness, but Mrs. Buttrick chuckled. "You'd best say your farewells. I believe the colonel is about to give orders."

Charlie greeted Hattie warmly, his blue eyes crinkling at the corners as he smiled, dark hair curling from under the brim of his brand-new kepi.

Teddy nudged Hattie. "The remembrance, remember?"

Hattie offered the cluster of roses, already drooping in the heat. Charlie stuck his drumsticks through the tight leather band on his drum. As soon as his white-gloved hand took the flowers from her, Hattie put her dirt-stained hands behind her back.

Charlie slipped the roses into the buttonhole at the collar of his crisp new jacket. The pale blossoms stood out against the blue wool. "Thank you, Hattie."

Teddy knelt to admire the eagle painted on the side

of Charlie's drum. "Have you learned all the commands?"

"Yes, indeed! March, halt, charge, assemble—nobody moves until we drum the order."

Teddy whistled. "You're the most important one in the whole company."

"Well, of course he is," came a bright voice behind Hattie. Lizzie Eisenmenger's hoops swayed above her ruffled drawers as she moved closer and tilted her head to gaze up at the drummer. "We wouldn't expect anything less of our Charlie."

The high crown of Lizzie's fashionable hat blocked Hattie's view as her classmate managed to slide in front of Hattie. "Charlie, dear, I've made a tussie-mussie just for you. Do you know the language of flowers?"

Before Charlie could answer, Lizzie continued, "Sweet William for gallantry, heliotrope for devotion, and ivy for enduring friendship. I hope you'll be a gallant soldier devoted to his duty—and to friends at home." Under her hat one of Lizzie's white-gloved fingers twisted a blonde curl. "When will you be coming home, Charlie?"

Hattie elbowed her way back into the circle. "These are the Hundred Days regiments, Lizzie. Everybody knows that. They'll be mustered out in September."

Lizzie gave Charlie a soulful glance and walked away, turning once to gaze at him over her shoulder.

Hattie looked at the bouquet in Charlie's hand. Red-and-white blossoms nestled among blue spikes of heliotrope. Tri-colored ribbons dangled from the ivy surrounding the lacy cone.

Charlie smiled at the wilting roses in his buttonhole.

"These flowers speak to me, too, Hattie," he said. "They speak of enduring friends devoted to base ball and gallantly . . . uh, gallantly . . ."

"Growing potatoes?" suggested Hattie.

"Exactly," said Charlie. "Gallantly growing potatoes while I go off to war. And minding the shop—isn't that right, Teddy?"

Hattie gaped at her brother. "You're taking Charlie's place at the shop?"

Teddy nodded. "Father told me last night."

"Just for the summer," said Charlie, putting his arm around Teddy's shoulders. "I expect to reclaim my position in September."

"Why didn't Father ask me? I'm older."

"You're a *girl*," said Teddy.

"It's a men's shop," added Charlie.

"But what about the garden, if Teddy's at the shop? It's not fair—"

At a sudden flurry among the officers Charlie thrust Lizzie's bouquet into the leather band of the drum and pulled out his drumsticks. He and the other musicians fell into line, and a lieutenant gave a sharp command. At the sound of the drums, the soldiers began to assemble. The last Hattie saw of Charlie Moores was Lizzie's ribbons fluttering from his drum.

July 1864

10.

THE AROMA of frying chicken wafted through the Bigelow kitchen as Hattie watched Ellen close the wicker luncheon basket. She and the other fifth and sixth graders at the Fourth Ward School had been excused from classes for a blackberry-picking expedition. Only the fact that Teddy was allowed to spend all day in Father's shop dampened Hattie's joy at the prospect of a school day without lessons.

"Now, darlin', mind you watch for snakes and such and stay well away from poison ivy. Leaves of three, as they say—leaves of three, leave them be."

"*Let* them be," came Miss Taft's firm voice as she walked into the kitchen wearing a striped cotton dress and carrying a straw hat.

Ellen snorted. "Let them or leave them, 'tis all one. And mind you don't eat so many berries that we have none for the dear soldiers."

The omnibus stood waiting in front of the Fourth Ward School, the sturdy gray horses switching their tails at flies. Hattie climbed narrow iron stairs to take a seat on the open vehicle and stowed the wicker basket under the long wooden bench.

When the draft horses pulled hard and the omnibus lurched forward, Hattie leaned one arm on the rail and watched the rows of houses in neat town lots give away to rambling farmyards surrounded by pastures and fields. At last the horses turned off the main road onto a rutted lane that curved along a pond shining among rolling hills.

Miss Taft stepped off the omnibus and ordered two boys to unload the stacks of tin pails. Hattie leaped to the ground from the top step, but Lizzie Eisenmenger descended slowly as her classmates admired the floral embroidery on her cream-colored boots.

Opening her parasol, Lizzie said, "Mama says I'll turn brown as a sailor if I don't stay out of the sun."

Those words made Hattie want to fling off her sunbonnet and spend the entire summer day bareheaded.

Lizzie stared at the empty pails. "I don't think I'll be able to carry a full pail all the way to the omnibus."

One of the boys stepped forward. "I'll help you," he said. Other boys jostled him aside. "No, let me—let me carry it!"

"*Chil*-dren," said Miss Taft firmly, "of course you may help one another, but I expect you all to do your share."

Hattie snatched her pail and strode off toward the thick brambles. She picked furiously, hardly pausing to eat any blackberries. Heedless of the thorns, she advanced like a soldier moving into enemy territory. Was this the way Charlie Moores felt when Colonel Buttrick gave the orders? Was the Thirty-ninth in danger at this very moment? She would pick more blackberries than anybody else to keep Charlie and his regiment safe and well.

When her pail was full, she climbed to the top of a green hill to look east toward the church steeples of Milwaukee silhouetted against the blue sky. At the faint ringing of Miss Taft's bell, she wound her way through the brambles to the meadow where quilts were laid on the grass for the picnic luncheon. As Hattie approached, Lizzie said loudly to Mary Ann, "Hattie's arms are all over scratches—I do think a young lady ought to keep herself tidier, don't you?"

Hattie set down her basket a good distance away from the girls. When George eyed her plate of fried chicken, she smiled and pushed the basket toward him. Eagerly he reached for the largest piece. By the time he finished a second piece and wiped his fingers on the grass, the other boys had dropped cotton napkins onto the grass for bases. Somebody called for George as the captains began choosing up sides.

George tossed the chicken bones aside and scrambled to his feet. Hattie packed up the basket and trotted out to the meadow. "Wait for me!"

The pitcher had taken his place within the diamond, ready to lob the first pitch.

Hattie looked from one captain to the other. "Which side should I play on?"

One of the boys snorted. "Base ball is a *gentleman's* game."

"I play in the yard at home." Hattie looked at George.

48

"Tell him I can play."

George merely looked down at his shoes.

"The teams are already even," called the pitcher. "Wouldn't be fair to add another player now."

"What isn't fair is that girls don't get to play." Hattie snatched up an empty pail and stormed back into the berry patch, heedless of anything that got in her way.

The next morning Hattie sat at the kitchen table rubbing furiously at the swollen red welts that dotted her arms. Some were beginning to ooze under the pale layer of salve that Ellen had applied to dry the sores and ease the itching.

"Mind you don't scratch," said Ellen without turning from the simmering kettle of blackberries. "You'll only make it worse. Fetch the jelly jars from the pantry. We'll make a fine batch of preserves for the regiment, and then you can write a letter to Charlie and tell him about your brave fight against those leaves of three."

Hattie sighed. "I should have left them be."

Ellen clicked her tongue. "*Let* them be."

11.

ON A SWELTERING AFTERNOON Hattie sat on the front porch making bandages with Lizzie and Mary Ann, while their mothers attended a meeting of the Soldiers' Home Society in the Bigelow parlor. After snipping a cut in the hem of a worn bed sheet, Hattie ripped a long strip a few inches wide, and dropped it into a pile. Lizzie and Mary Ann wrapped each of the strips neatly around an old broomstick, then slipped the rolls off and added them to the basket of bandages on the floor.

Lizzie smiled at Mary Ann. "I'm glad that you and I were given this task. I don't believe that clumsy hands could manage such delicate work."

Hattie tugged fiercely at her length of sheet—*Rrrrip!*

Through the open window Mother called, "Girls, you're doing a lovely job out there. You'll want to listen to this next item of business—Missus Hewitt is going to read Missus Buttrick's letter from Memphis."

Hattie stopped ripping so she could hear.

> "*My dear Mrs. Hewitt,*
> *The box came this afternoon and what a happy time we had opening it! We had it carried to the rear of the hospital tent . . . The convalescents drew shyly near to get a peek*

*. . . Thank Mr. Hewitt for his fans, the boys
all wanted one, thinking no doubt that a few
whiffs of Old Lake Michigan might be hidden
in their folds."*

Mrs. Buttrick hardly mentioned any military actions. Most of her letter consisted of thanking the residents of Milwaukee for their contributions to the Hundred Days regiment assembled from their fair city.

*"My best compliments to Mr. Bell. Tell him I
have not words to thank him for his invaluable
donation . . . My love and many thanks to little
Hattie Bigelow—"*

Hattie looked up in surprise.

*"—for her jar of beautiful jelly. It made me
quite hungry to look at it."*

Lizzie whispered, "I don't see that there's anything special about a jar of jelly. Most of the soldiers won't get even a lick of it."

Hattie held the bed sheet in her hands directly in front of Lizzie, ripping with such vigor that the strip flew into Lizzie's face.

"Hattie!"

At Mother' voice through the window, Hattie turned meekly around. "Yes, ma'am?"

A hand held a sealed envelope over the sill. "When you

finish your work, you may open this letter."

Hattie took the precious envelope in both hands and read "C. Moores" in one corner. She set the letter on the window sill and set to tearing the sheet furiously till a mound of strips lay at her feet. Without another word to Lizzie or Mary Ann, she used her scissors to slit open the envelope. Then Hattie leaped off the porch and galloped around the house to the back yard to sit alone in the cool shade of the lilacs.

Carefully she pulled the folded page from the envelope and flattened it open on her lap.

> *Dear Mr. & Mrs. Bigelow, Hattie & Teddy,*
>
> *Here in Memphis the days are always hot—the air along the river is still and close, and some men have been taken ill with fever. However, the heat could not keep us from celebrating Independence Day. We fashioned our own equipment for a base ball game in a sheep pasture. One of the men spent considerable time carving a bat from a hickory branch. To make a ball, we wrapped strips of woolen cloth around a walnut, and sewed the leather from one fellow's old brogans into a covering.*
>
> *Mrs. Buttrick cheered gallantly for both sides—any good play seemed to win her favor. You must tell Mr. Jenkins that I even hit a home run!*
>
> *We ended our 4th of July with a parade of giants. Six soldiers hoisted smaller men onto*

their shoulders. The top men wrapped themselves in blankets to cover the heads of the men below. Billy the fifer and I led the procession through the camp to the tunes of "Yankee Doodle" and the "Battle Hymn of the Republic." How I wish you could have seen it, for it was a jolly sight.

Camp life goes from pure fun to drudgery, but I am proud to do my duty here. I trust that Teddy is keeping the shop in good order until my return.

Ever yours,
Charles Moores

August 1864

12.

ON A HOT AND MUGGY MORNING Mother stood on the porch surveying the garden as Hattie sat on the steps beside a basket half-full of green beans.

Mother eyed the basket. "I told Missus Hewitt I'd have beans for the Soldiers' Home today. You haven't picked nearly enough."

With a sigh Hattie said, "I picked all the beans I could."

"That's not true. From where I stand, I can see more beans in that second row."

Hattie shrugged. "Can't pick those beans till the day after tomorrow. That's Teddy's moon row."

"What the goodness does that mean?"

Hattie pointed to the garden. "See the moon carved on the picket? He planted that row by the moon's phase, so he needs to harvest by the moon's phase. You put *us* in charge of the garden, remember?"

Mother folded her arms. "That's quite enough, Hattie. Since Teddy is working at the shop, *you* can harvest *his* row right now."

"It's not fair that I'm working like a slave in this garden while Teddy gets to go downtown and work in the shop."

"Hattie Bigelow, do *not* use that word so lightly. Our Union soldiers are sacrificing their lives to end slavery."

Hattie stared at the ground. "I'm sorry."

"Now pick more beans for the boys who made it home."

Hattie trudged back to the garden, straddled Teddy's row of beans, and started picking, the hot sun blazing on her back. She hardly looked up when she heard George approach.

"Teddy isn't here. He's working in the *shop*."

George bent down to peer among the vines in the next row. "Cucumbers are ready to pick."

"How can that be? I just picked them the other day." Hattie brushed aside the prickly vines, uncovering a huge yellow cucumber. She plucked it from the vine and pitched it across the yard.

"What are you doing?" cried George, running to retrieve the smashed cucumber.

"Ellen says the old ones are tough and full of seeds." Hattie carried the basket of beans to the porch. "But I'll catch it from Mother if she sees I've let the cucumbers go to waste." She glanced about the yard. "I've got to get rid of them."

"I'll help you pick," said George, "and I'll take the old ones to my house."

"What will you do with them? Use them for batting practice?"

George shrugged. "I'll figure out something."

Hattie wiped her sweaty face with a corner of her pinafore and picked up a peck basket. "Let's get to work."

A summer storm brought some relief from the heat, and on Sunday afternoon Hattie and Teddy tiptoed through the muddy garden, stepping over the thick stems and broad leaves of the spreading muskmelon vines. From the edge of the garden Ellen said, "Take hold of a good one and give it a wee tug."

Hattie grasped a large melon and tugged gently. "It's not coming off."

Teddy reached into his pocket. "I'll cut it loose."

"No, 'tisn't ripe if you can't tug it loose."

Hattie pulled at another melon and smiled as it popped off the vine.

"We'll take a fine treat to the boys at the Soldiers' Home," Ellen said. "Fetch your wagon, boyo."

Teddy straightened up in dismay. "Are we giving away all our melons?"

Ellen chuckled. "Don't you fret now. We'll feast on melons for a week."

As Hattie continued her search for ripe melons, the shrill voices of the Moores girls sounded from the sidewalk. "Hattie, Hattie! Come and see!"

The tops of two white parasols peeked over the fence. Hattie set the melon on the grass and walked past rows of potatoes and carrots and onions to the gate.

Molly and Bea smiled up at her in their Sunday dresses, their faces rosy under the shade of the open parasols.

"Look at the ribbons, Hattie!" said Bea. "Mine are pink like Lizzie's."

Molly nodded. "And mine are blue like my eyes."

Hattie wiped her dirty hands on her pinafore. "They're beautiful. Where did you get them?"

The little girls answered so fast she could hardly keep track of who was speaking.

"Before he left, Charlie said that Mama should have all his pay, but he wrote that he wanted to buy something for us—"

"Whatever our hearts desired!"

"Mama took us downtown and let us choose!"

Bea sighed rapturously. "It's so fine to look like a lady."

Molly twirled her parasol. "We want to go out walking, but Mama only allows us to go 'round the block, and all the neighbors have seen us already."

"Please, Hattie," said Bea, "won't you take us walking?"

Hattie looked down at her soiled pinafore and muddy boots. "I'm making a delivery to the Soldiers' Home. If you ask your mother, you can come along with me."

By the time Hattie had cleaned her boots and washed up, the Moores girls were waiting impatiently at the gate. Teddy had loaded the melons into the wagon and then disappeared to George's house. Even when he wasn't at the boot and shoe shop, he managed to avoid garden work.

Hattie and Molly and Bea set off down the sidewalk, the little girls walking grandly ahead and Hattie pulling the small wagon behind. As they passed each house, Molly and Bea called "Good afternoon!" to every person sitting out on a front porch. Hattie decided there was no point in telling the girls that ladies were not supposed to call out to strangers.

The construction site at St. Gall's was empty and quiet on this Sunday afternoon, and only a few wagons and buggies were parked along West Water Street. Yet outside the front door of the Soldiers' Home a crowd of soldiers and civilians stood talking loudly and earnestly. Molly and Bea stopped, unable to make their way through the group of men, and Hattie said, "Pardon me" several times, but nobody seemed to listen.

She heard snatches of conversation. "Forrest's raiders" and "barely escaped" and "five hundred prisoners." And finally . . . "attacking Memphis."

Memphis.

Hattie dropped the handle of the wagon and touched the sleeve of one of the soldiers. "Please, sir, what happened in Memphis?"

"Why, Memphis was raided before dawn! Forrest attacked—his cavalry tore up and down the town."

"What happened to our regiments? What about the Thirty-ninth?"

Another soldier snorted. "Those green recruits? I said it was a fool plan to replace seasoned troops with Hundred Days men. And I'm sorry to be proved right."

"The forest!" whimpered Bea. "Did a forest attack Charlie's company?"

"No," said Molly slowly, "the Rebs did."

13.

When Mr. Jenkins came home the next evening, Hattie abandoned her weeding and joined him on the porch.

"Have you heard any news from Memphis?"

Mr. Jenkins settled into a wicker chair and opened the newspaper. "From what I've heard, the Thirty-ninth sustained very few casualties. Here's the article—General Nathan Bedford Forrest and his men rode into Memphis in an attempt to capture Union generals and free the Confederate prisoners from Irving prison." Mr. Jenkins chuckled. "It seems that all Forrest got for his efforts was General Washburn's coat, as Washburn escaped just ahead of him."

"So the Thirty-ninth wasn't involved?"

"Not in the main raid—though there were skirmishes all around Memphis."

"I'll feel better if we actually hear from Charlie—or anybody in the regiment."

Mr. Jenkins nodded. "Many a household is waiting for news."

Hattie's world shrank again to the size of the garden in which she spent hours each day. On one rare afternoon that Teddy was home, the two faced one another in one of the "moon rows," stooping to snap green beans from the stems. Deep in the shade of the lilacs, Molly and Bea were having a tea party with their dolls. Occasionally Hattie could hear the high voices of fine ladies with grand manners over the drone of the insects and the chirping of birds.

"I'll race you to the middle," said Teddy.

"It's not a contest," Hattie said without looking up. "And you miss too many when you pick fast."

"I do or you do?" asked Teddy. "I haven't been picking."

Hattie did not bother to answer. She was not pleased to see George Schaefer enter the yard. She stood up and said crossly, "No, George, Teddy can't come and play. He'd best pick well enough that he doesn't leave a mess of stringy tough beans for the next picking."

Teddy reached down through the leaves and pulled out a handful of overgrown bean pods. "See? You're the one who hasn't been picking well." He flung the old beans out of the garden.

"Maybe if I didn't have to work alone here hour after hour I'd be able to get them all."

George stared at the scattering of yellow pods on the grass.

The porch door creaked open, and Mother called, "Children, I've brought Missus Hewitt's letter from Missus Buttrick!"

Hattie and Teddy hastily brushed the dirt from their hands and approached the house, George trailing slowly after them. Molly and Bea burst from the leaves clutching their dolls. The five children settled onto the porch steps as Mother sat down in the rocking chair, her hoops ballooning up before she settled them into place. Unfolding the letter, she began to read:

> "My dear Mrs. Hewitt,
> You have doubtless heard about General Forrest's great raid into Memphis? Our boys did not see all of it that they wanted to but I felt that they had seen enough when I looked upon the wounded . . ."

Mother glanced at the little Moores girls and hesitated before continuing. "Never mind that bit." She ran her finger down the letter. "Here's the part about Missus Buttrick." She read on:

> "As soon as it was broad day light, I went over to camp and cooked breakfast for headquarters with the cannon roaring in my ears and the balls flying overhead. It was grand. I enjoyed it ever so much. I wish you had been there."

"But what does she say about the rest of the regiment?" Hattie asked.

Mother skimmed the rest of the letter. "Five of our boys taken prisoner—none that we know . . . she fears the accounts of the raid have been exaggerated here, and hopes we are not anxious . . . she has sent three of the boys to the Home. They arrived yesterday."

"So is Charlie a hero because the forest didn't get him?" asked Bea.

"All of the Hundred Days men are heroes," said Molly.

George snorted. "Heroes? All they were supposed to do is keep the Rebs out of Memphis—and they couldn't even do that." His voice was harsh. "All the real soldiers are in Virginia with General Grant. Or on the way to Atlanta with General Sherman."

Teddy bristled. "Are you saying that Charlie isn't a real soldier?"

"I'm saying all we hear is that he's playing base ball in Memphis—isn't that what he wrote you in his letter?"

Hattie crossed her arms. "Charlie's doing his part just like the rest of us."

"Well, my father is with the real soldiers. He's part of the Iron Brigade. And they sure ain't wasting their time playing *base ball*." George stomped away, but suddenly halted to pick up the discarded beans.

Hattie had heard her father and Mr. Jenkins talk of the Iron Brigade, which was the pride of Wisconsin, a tough unit of men who had fought many battles since the beginning of the war.

Hattie heard a sniffle and turned to see tears rolling down Bea's face.

"Don't listen to him," Hattie said fiercely.

"But he's right," Bea sobbed. "Charlie was playing base ball when the raiders came. Missus Buttrick was cooking breakfast with balls flying overhead."

September 1864

14.

O N THE DAY that Thirty-ninth was to return to Milwaukee, Hattie was allowed to assist Teddy at the boot and shoe shop while the two of them waited for the arrival of the troop train. Pausing with her dust rag in one hand and a pair of brogans in the other, Hattie glared at her younger brother. "You needn't watch me so. I am perfectly capable of dusting the shelves!"

She set the brogans neatly beside the others and moved toward the next set of shelves. Here the boots were in disarray, not even lined up in pairs. Hattie picked up a boot and searched for its mate. She set it down and picked up another.

"Father, none of these boots match! The whole shelf is all mixed up."

Father cleared his throat. "Those are boots for returning soldiers."

"Don't returning soldiers need matching boots?"

Teddy folded his arms. "Don't you know anything? Some of them come home with only one leg."

Hattie shoved the boot back onto the shelf. "I know more than you do about returning soldiers. I'm the one who delivers supplies to the Home."

Father reached into his vest pocket for his watch and clicked open the lid. "You two may leave for the station. Be sure to stay well away from the sick ones—your mother heard that some of the men have caught river fever."

The children hurried through the streets bustling with other Milwaukeeans walking in the same direction. Yet as the crowd neared the railroad station, the onlookers grew quieter.

Hattie and Teddy scurried around the edges of the crowd, standing on tiptoe and craning their necks, until they saw a line of wagons in front of the platform. A woman in a cloak and bonnet directed a group of soldiers who were carrying a number of blanketed forms on stretchers toward the wagons.

Hattie recognized the figure and pointed her out to Teddy. "She seems to be the only one who knows what to do." She could not resist calling, "Welcome home, Missus Buttrick! Is Charlie safe?"

The woman glanced up at the greeting. "Yes, he is, but I have twenty invalids here, and we haven't enough beds at the Home. Could you run to there for me? I've sent Captain Osborne out to Camp Washburn to fetch pallets." She pulled a folded paper from her drawstring bag. "The beds must be moved to make room—I've written out instructions for Missus Hewitt." She handed the note to Hattie.

"Yes, ma'am. I'll take it there directly."

As soon as Mrs. Buttrick turned back toward the soldiers, Teddy whispered, "Mother said not to go to the Soldiers' Home."

Hattie held up the paper. "She didn't know I'd be needed to carry a message."

"What about the fever?"

Already pushing her way through the crowd, Hattie called back over her shoulder, "Be sure to watch for Charlie! I'll meet you back at the shop."

After running all the way from the station, Hattie burst into the Soldiers' Home, startling Private Mackenzie and another soldier sitting near the front windows. "Where's Missus Hewitt?" she gasped.

Before either of them could answer, Missus Hewitt stepped out from the back room. "Hattie Bigelow, what on earth are you doing here?"

Panting, Hattie handed over the note and leaned forward with her hands on her knees to catch her breath. "Missus Buttrick needs you to make room for more sick soldiers."

"Dear Fanny, she's even drawn a diagram—but how are we going to move all these beds?"

"We can help, ma'am," said Private Mackenzie. "That's what we did in the field hospitals. Those on the mend would help as they could."

Hattie straightened up. "I'm very strong. If someone can get the men out of bed, I can move the beds into position." She walked to the nearest empty bed, grabbed the iron footboard with both hands, and shifted the frame a few feet.

"You shouldn't be here at all," said Mrs. Hewitt, "but you may help for a few minutes. Stay well away from the fever cases—those are the beds at the far end of the room. Private Mackenzie, could you and the matron assist the invalids? Private Cline, please help to move the beds."

Under Mrs. Hewitt's direction, Hattie and the soldier shifted beds tightly end to end. There would be no walking in a hoop skirt down the narrowed aisles. Hattie politely averted her eyes from the sick and wounded men. She and Private Cline were still moving beds when the first hospital wagon pulled up outside.

Mrs. Hewitt started for the door. "Hattie, please go upstairs and move the beds in the north room. Those are all empty, so you shouldn't need help."

"Yes, ma'am." After glimpsing the haggard men downstairs, Hattie did not mind that Mrs. Hewitt wanted to prevent her from seeing the incoming soldiers of the Thirty-ninth.

By the time she set the last bed into place, she was dripping with sweat. She turned at the sound of footsteps to face a woman in the doorway—Mother.

"Hattie Bigelow, what the goodness are you doing here? I expressly forbade you to come!" Mother seized her arm so tightly Hattie winced. "Don't you understand that men are *dying* here? We have already bought plots for their graves—this is no place for a young girl. Get home at once!"

15.

FOR TWO DAYS after the regiment returned, Hattie and Teddy barely saw Mother at all. In the kitchen Ellen murmured prayers for the souls of the poor boys newly buried in the Soldiers' Home plot at Forest Home Cemetery.

On the afternoon that Charlie was to be mustered out, Hattie told Ellen she would go sit on the Moores porch to wait for him to arrive home.

"That you won't, darlin'. Think of his mother now—we must give her and those little sisters a stretch of time alone with their dear one. Tomorrow is soon enough for the likes of us."

Hattie sighed and went out to the garden to haul weeds to the pile beside the outhouse. But when shrieks erupted from the Moores yard, she could not resist peeking through the hedge to see Molly and Bea run to Charlie, still in uniform, who lifted them both in an exuberant hug and spun them completely around, their skirts swirling like flowers. He set them down and they clung to his legs, and his weeping mother embraced him as if she would never let go.

Hattie stepped slowly back from the lilacs and turned toward her garden.

The next day Miss Taft called a meeting of the sixth grade girls after school, and Hattie slumped in her seat as Lizzie Eisenmenger talked on and on about the sewing circle's plan to provide a table of fancy work for the upcoming dinner and dance at Birchard's Hall. Knowing that Teddy had been excused from work at the shop today to visit Charlie made Lizzie's chatter of ribbons and laces almost unendurable. At last Miss Taft dismissed the girls, and Hattie charged out of the classroom, down the stairwell, and out the door.

She ran so fast she was nearly breathless by the time she saw Charlie, no longer in uniform, playing catch in his front yard with Teddy and George. Charlie was so intent on the game that he did not see her until Molly called, "Hattie, Hattie—d'you see? Charlie's home!"

He caught Teddy's throw and turned toward her. His face was thinner, his nose and cheeks burnt browner than she had ever seen.

"Welcome home, Charlie," she said, her voice quavering unexpectedly. Wishing furiously that she could run to him the way his sisters had, she stood still, unable to think of anything else to say.

When he smiled, his eyes were not as merry as she remembered. Drawing back his arm, he said "Can you still catch?" and lobbed the ball high into the air.

Hattie moved swiftly into position, hands ready. The smack of the leather stung her palms, but she raised the ball in triumph.

"Well done, Hattie!"

She blushed at his praise.

He glanced toward the Bigelow yard. "I surely missed our neighborhood. Wish we could hit a few on the old diamond."

Eagerly Hattie said, "We could do that if we're careful. Get the bat, Teddy! It'll be just like old times." She led the way through the hedge, and Charlie surveyed the yard. "I don't see how we can play base ball in a garden."

"We've harvested the cabbage and onions, so it's safe to walk along here. Just stay away from the pumpkin vines over there."

Charlie looked dubiously down the staked rows. "Where's home plate?"

"Right around here," said Hattie, gesturing toward the potatoes.

Teddy stepped surefootedly through the garden with the bat. "You pitch, Charlie. I'll be the first striker."

"I'll catch," said George quickly.

Hattie opened her mouth to protest, then said, "I'll take the outfield, but I want to be the second striker."

From the edge of the yard she watched Charlie and Teddy try to stand where the pitcher and striker had always stood, but they had to shift positions so neither of them would straddle a row of potatoes.

Charlie shook his head. "It doesn't feel the same."

"Pitch it to me, Charlie!" Teddy waved the bat in the air.

Teddy got his hit, and Hattie scrambled through the lilacs for the ball, the leaves rattling against her skirts. She threw the ball to Charlie, who watched Teddy lope around the garden, leaping rows as he traced the outline of the old base-ball diamond.

"It's my turn!" Hattie trotted toward home plate and picked up the bat.

"Things surely have changed around here," Charlie muttered. He walked over to a bare spot in the garden. "Hattie, stand over there to strike."

Hattie felt odd facing the fence instead of the lilacs. "We never used to line up this way."

"Just hit the ball."

As the ball sailed toward her, Hattie swung the bat ferociously and missed.

Behind her, George scampered after the ball, snickering.

"Oh, *hush, George!*" Hattie said through clenched teeth. She tried to remember Mr. Jenkins' advice last spring. Shifting her grip on the bat, she waited for the pitch, and when it came, her swing smacked the ball up and out of bounds and—*crash!*

Hattie dropped the bat, staring in horror at the shattered window in the garden shed.

October 1864

16.

HATTIE THRUST THE GARDEN FORK deep into the earth to pry up another cluster of potatoes. She flung her load to the grass, where Teddy shook off the dirt and added the potatoes to a heaping bushel.

"I'm cold," said Teddy. "Can we quit now?"

"You should have been here in the heat of summer," said Hattie. "Then you'd be thankful for this cool air." She dug deeper and flung each load harder, making Teddy scramble to collect the scattered potatoes.

"That's quite an arm you have, Hattie Bigelow. The regiment could have used your help digging trenches in Memphis."

She turned to see Charlie leaning over the gate. He had not visited the Bigelows since the ball game in the garden two weeks ago. His thin face wore a crooked half-smile.

Hattie turned away. "Shouldn't you be working in Father's shop?" she said coldly, stabbing her fork into the ground.

"Your father has given me the afternoon off to help set up for the dinner and dance tonight."

Hattie snorted. "I suppose Father considers that his contribution to the cause."

"Did you get in trouble for the broken window? I told your father it was my fault, and that he should take the cost from my wages."

"After Mother *and* Father *and* Ellen *and* Miss Taft all scolded me."

Teddy stood watching them anxiously. "Here, Charlie!" He lobbed a potato, which Charlie caught easily and tossed right back.

"Let me help you haul that bushel, Teddy." Charlie leaped the fence and took one handle while Teddy struggled manfully with the other, barely able to lift his side.

Hattie walked ahead to open the slanted cellar door alongside the house. Charlie took the basket, grunting as he stepped heavily down the rough stairs. A few potatoes tilted out, thumping and bumping to the dirt floor. Charlie set the potatoes beside heaping bushels of turnips, beets, carrots, and squash. He whistled. "That's quite a harvest."

Teddy picked up a potato. "I think Ellen's potatoes and Miss Taft's look about the same."

Hattie considered. "Then Ellen's grew faster because they were planted later."

Charlie sat down on the wooden step. "Do you mean to tell me that *Miss Taft* planted potatoes, too?"

Hattie stamped her foot. "*I* was the one who weeded and watered and harvested while the regiment was away and Teddy was at the shop and Miss Taft was nagging about sewing circles! Why should everybody else get credit for *my* harvest?"

"It's *not* all yours," said Teddy. "I planted right alongside you."

Charlie stood up. "Well, your father didn't give me the afternoon off to gad about. I'd best be going."

Hattie and Teddy followed him up the stairs. Charlie stood for a moment gazing at his house on the other side of the lilac hedge. "Plenty of nights in Memphis, Hattie, I went to bed wishing I could taste home cooking and watch the moon rise over the lilacs." He flexed his shoulders. "I'll see you tonight at Birchard's Hall."

17.

THAT EVENING Hattie and her family arrived early at Birchard's Hall, the largest gathering place in the Fourth Ward. They climbed up the stairs past Mr. Birchard's shops on the first floor and offices on the second floor to the ballroom on the third floor. As she trotted from the back room to the main room, placing plates of oysters on the tables for eager guests, Hattie decided that Father and Mr. Jenkins looked splendid in their coats and tails. She was disappointed that Colonel Buttrick was no longer in uniform, but Mrs. Buttrick looked as regal as a queen with a glittering necklace above the familiar rose silk gown.

Hattie hardly had time to admire the dresses or the guests, for the moment she returned to the back room Ellen or Mrs. Moores would hand her a new dish to serve. "I hope there's something left for me to eat," she muttered with an envious glance at Teddy, who was digging into a plate of roast beef.

After the guests finished supper, Hattie and half a dozen other girls cleared away the plates and glasses and silverware and snatched off the tablecloths moments before Charlie and his crew hauled the tables out of the way for dancing. On the stage the quadrille band tuned up as the men conversed in twos and threes, a mix of blue uniforms and black frock coats. On the other side of the room clusters of young women in pale dresses whispered and giggled. Lizzie Eisenmenger walked daintily among the ladies with a lace-edged basket, handing out dance cards.

At the table piled with fancy needlework by the West Side women and girls, the guests showed their support for the Union cause by purchasing embroidered comb cases and other finery.

Colonel Buttrick led Missus Buttrick toward the stage to take their places as the head couple.

"Do you see that?" said a voice behind Hattie.

Hattie turned to face Lizzie Eisenmenger, who said, "I can't believe Missus Buttrick is wearing a turned dress. We've seen that rose silk for years. The Buttricks can afford to keep a carriage, after all, so I don't understand why she would wear the same shabby gown."

Hattie bristled. "Missus Buttrick would rather buy supplies for the Soldiers' Home than silk for a new dress. I think she looks beautiful."

"I'm sure you do," said Lizzie, "but nobody expects the kitchen crew to know much about fashion."

Her pointed stare made Hattie realize she was still wearing a stained pinafore over her best crimson dress. Hastily she ducked into the back room.

"There you are, darlin'," said Ellen, handing her a dish towel. "Many hands make light work, as they say."

While Hattie dried plates, she listened to the fiddles playing the Grand March.

Teddy and Charlie wandered into the back room, and Ellen offered them more apple tarts.

Hattie stacked the last of the plates, slipped off her pinafore, and gazed longingly out at the dance floor.

Mrs. Moores, a plump woman with dark hair and blue eyes just like Charlie's, said cheerfully, "Hattie Bigelow, in a few years I daresay your dance card will always be full. And soon after we'll see Teddy in the Grand March as well."

Teddy licked his fingers and shook his head. "The only marching I want to do is in a regiment."

Charlie grinned. "A soldier needs to know his way around a ballroom. It's a gentleman's duty to please the ladies."

Teddy straightened up indignantly. "I do know my way around a ballroom." He turned to Hattie. "Good evening, Miss Bigelow. If you are not otherwise engaged, might I have the pleasure of this dance?" He crooked his right elbow, his expression so serious that Hattie stifled her laugh and slipped her arm through his.

As Teddy escorted her through the room, Charlie and his mother fell into step behind them. The band in the main hall struck up the opening bars of "Soldiers' Joy," and the two couples promenaded to the door. Teddy turned left and Hattie turned right to march around the room while Ellen and the kitchen crew clapped time.

Hattie met Teddy again, and they turned about to face the others. She found herself beaming at Charlie as the four of them took hands and circled left, then circled right. She and Charlie ended up spinning in a two-hand swing, and the dancers romped to a finish. Curtseying to Teddy, then to Charlie, Hattie was giddy with delight.

November 1864

18.

ON THE FIRST MONDAY IN NOVEMBER the Fourth Ward School was abuzz with excitement—a torchlight procession was to wind through downtown Milwaukee in support of General McClellan, the Union officer who was running for president. Hattie was dismayed to hear how many of her classmates seemed to favor Lincoln's challenger in the coming election. On the way home from school even George said confidently, "General McClellan's our man. Mac will win the Union back."

Hattie bristled. "Lincoln is fighting to preserve the Union."

"Yes, but McClellan wants peace."

"So does Lincoln!"

Teddy broke in. "That's not what he means, Hattie. George means McClellan's party wants to negotiate for peace right now."

George smirked. "Girls don't understand politics."

"I understand perfectly," said Hattie. "If McClellan is elected, he'll save the Union. But there will still be slaves.

Lincoln is committed to winning the war and ending slavery forever."

"And how many years will that take?" said George. He thrust his hands into his pockets and walked furiously ahead.

Too late Hattie remembered the father, serving on the front lines in the Iron Brigade, that George had seen only once in the last three years.

That evening Hattie and Teddy were startled to see Mr. Jenkins sitting at the kitchen table as Ellen cleared his plate, humming a cheerful tune.

He smiled at their confusion. "Ellen served me an early supper—now I must head back into town." He slipped into his gray overcoat, wrapped a red muffler around his neck, and picked up his bowler hat. "Thank you, Ellen. Good night, children."

After the back door closed behind Mr. Jenkins, Teddy said, "We ought to go downtown and help Father guard the shop."

"Guard the shop?"

He nodded. "Father said that some men might cause trouble on Election Eve. Mother and some of the other ladies are staying late at the Soldiers' Home to establish a proper moral tone."

Ellen chuckled. "You sound like such a little man, boyo. Sit down to supper, both of you, whilst I run this tray up to Miss Taft. Then we'll put on our coats and go downtown."

Hattie stared at Ellen. "But the parade is for General McClellan. You don't support him, do you?"

Ellen pursed her lips. "Whist now, all of St. Gall's will turn out to see the fun. I shouldn't like to miss it. There won't be such an occasion for another four years."

Glad of her warm coat and gloves, Hattie hurried along the dark street between Teddy and Ellen.

"Teddy, why do you think Miss Taft said she would leave the speeches to those who vote?"

"She knows ladies don't need to worry about politics. Women don't run businesses or fight in wars."

"That's not true! The West Side ladies run the Soldiers' Home, and Missus Buttrick went to Memphis with the regiment."

"Yes, but their husbands do the voting."

"But what if a wife doesn't agree with her husband?" She thought of Miss Taft and Ellen. "And what about women who aren't married? Ellen, do you think women should vote?"

Teddy whooped with laughter at the notion, and Ellen said, "Darlin', I'll never live to see the day."

"I surely hope I will," Hattie muttered, and the three walked in silence for a time.

As they neared the riverfront, they were surrounded by a gathering crowd of men, women, and even small children with faces full of wonder at this adventure in the dark. Several times Ellen called out "Good evening" to acquaintances, but Hattie did not see any of Mother's or Father's friends.

The porches of the houses along the parade route were strung with paper lanterns glowing red and blue and green. A golden aura shone through lace curtains in the front rooms. From upper-story windows the residents waved and called out to friends below.

Many of the storefront windows featured large signs, some hand-lettered, others professionally printed. Hattie stopped smiling when she read the words outside a butcher shop—"*Old Abe removed McClellan, We'll now remove Old Abe.*"

Rattling drums and snatches of verse echoed off the brick buildings further down the street.

> "*Hurrah, hurrah for little Mac,*
> *For he's the one to win the Union back,*
> *And sail the ship of state on safer track.*
> *Hurrah! Hurrah for Little Mac!*"

Hattie turned to Ellen. "You were humming that song in the kitchen!"

"Sure, and 'tis a catchy tune, after all."

The procession turned the corner, led by dozens of men holding torches on long poles. Flames leaped high into the sky, and the cream-colored bricks reflected the torchlight. As the first row of marchers drew near the bridge, Hattie could read the slogan printed on the lanterns—"*Mac will win the Union back.*" Other men sang and chanted, waving their arms in time and encouraging the onlookers to join them. The men in the crowd responded with applause, cheering and whistling and bellowing out the song.

Another line of torchbearers led a group of men in bowler hats sporting red, white and blue rosettes pinned to their coats. "Those must be the speakers," Teddy said. "They'll work to stir up the crowd when the parade ends in the city square."

Hattie looked closer at the men most responsible for getting votes for McClellan. She stared in disbelief at a familiar figure with a red muffler bright above the rosette. "That's Mister Jenkins!" As the marchers crossed the bridge she watched the reflected flames twisting and writhing in the dark water, a nightmarish procession. If even Mr. Jenkins was casting his vote for the enemy, how could President Lincoln ever win the election?

On Election Day Hattie's classes seemed unbearably long, and she grimaced to hear Lizzie Eisenmenger's account of waving her handkerchief from a balcony. On the way home from school George was smug about the prospect of McClellan winning.

"Never!" Hattie said with a confidence she did not feel.

When Mr. Jenkins came home late that evening, Hattie ignored his greeting as he took off his coat and hung up his red muffler. "Is something wrong, Hattie?"

"I don't understand why Mother and Father allow you to stay in our house."

He raised his eyebrows. "Those are strong words. Are you upset because McClellan won the Milwaukee vote? Is this what's bothering you?"

"Does that mean Lincoln will lose the election?"

"We don't know yet. All of the states must submit their totals to be tallied in Washington. The telegraph office may get the results late tonight."

"How could you speak against President Lincoln?"

"Hattie, an election isn't about personalities. It's about possible solutions to the country's problems. I want the war to end so George's father can come home. I want the fighting to stop before the Southern states are completely destroyed."

"But what about the slaves?"

"I believe that with a negotiated peace, slavery will be abolished eventually."

Hattie shook her head. "I believe we ought to keep fighting to free the slaves. That's the only real way to support the Union."

Hattie woke from a fitful dream of torches and drums and the chant—"*Mac will win the Union back.*" Her eyes fluttered open—she still heard a drumbeat. She scrambled out of bed under the slanted ceiling, calling for Teddy to wake up, and struggled to push up the window sash. Cold air blew through her flannel gown and Teddy's nightshirt as they stared at the moonlit garden far below, where Charlie Moores stood with his drum.

"Lincoln re-elected!" he called, punctuating the report with a quick tattoo.

Hattie stuck her head out the window and shouted for all the world to hear. "Hurrah! Hurrah for Honest Abe!"

19.

O N THANKSGIVING DAY the entire house was fragrant with the aroma of the pumpkin pies that Hattie and Mother loaded carefully into the pie baskets. Several of the West Side families were to share a holiday dinner at Birchard's Hall with the residents of the Soldiers' Home.

"I hope I don't have to spend the entire evening serving and cleaning up," Hattie said.

"That is no way to talk. Everyone will help out tonight."

"Even Teddy? Even Miss Taft—and Mister Jenkins?" Since the election, Hattie had avoided Mr. Jenkins.

"Miss Taft and Mister Jenkins have accepted invitations elsewhere. But the Schaefers will be joining us. Run and get ready now—it's time to go."

At Birchard's Hall, Private Mackenzie and some of the other soldiers had set up tables and chairs at one end of the long room. Lizzie Eisenmenger was arranging vases of asters and mums for the tables. When Mother suggested that Hattie help to set the tables, Hattie said quickly, "I expect Ellen needs help with the food. Teddy can do it."

"That's girls' work," said Teddy.

"Not in the army," said Private Mackenzie. "In camp, everyone pitches in." He held out his arm. "Here, I'll lend you a hand."

Teddy stifled a laugh, and Mother frowned at him. Private Mackenzie grinned and picked up a plate.

In the back room, Hattie put pickled beets into glass dishes and carried them to the tables. Mrs. Vedder was carving the turkeys, and Mrs. Eisenmenger filled platters with spicy sausages while Ellen mashed the largest pot of potatoes that Hattie had ever seen.

By the time Father and Colonel Buttrick and the rest of the soldiers arrived, Hattie had made several trips back and forth with covered dishes and platters. When Mrs. Buttrick announced that dinner was served, Hattie looked for a place to sit.

She was about to sit next to Teddy when she saw Lizzie Eisenmenger standing behind an empty chair between Mrs. Eisenmenger and Private Mackenzie. Lizzie stared at the soldier's empty sleeve and said, "I don't want to sit here."

Immediately Hattie strode to the table and elbowed Lizzie aside. "This is *my* seat. You'll have to sit with Teddy and George."

Hattie settled into the chair next to Private Mackenzie. "Those sausages certainly smell good, Missus Eisenmenger," she said with a smile.

Mrs. Buttrick clapped her hands, and the room fell silent. "I'm sure you have all read President Lincoln's Thanksgiving Proclamation. Here in Milwaukee we have been truly blessed. As I look about this hall, I give thanks to the soldiers here and elsewhere who pledge their lives to the cause of freedom and humanity. I give thanks to the lady managers of the Soldiers' Home and to our community for their generous contributions." She looked down the table. "I give thanks to those who prepared our dinner this evening—and to Lizzie Eisenmenger, who decorated our tables so artfully—"

Hattie could see Lizzie beaming.

"—and to Hattie Bigelow, whose garden supplied our potatoes and beets and pumpkin pies."

Private Mackenzie nudged Hattie with the stub of his arm. "Well done."

". . . and now let us rise up to sing praise."

The scraping of chairs was drowned out by Colonel Buttrick's baritone voice in the opening lines: *Come, ye thankful people, come, raise the song of harvest home—"*

By the end of the first verse all of the guests joined in singing the favorite hymn.

When they took their seats again, the room echoed with the clinking of serving spoons on china as the dishes were passed around.

"George Schaefer," said Lizzie from the next table, "why are you gobbling so? Doesn't anybody feed you at home?"

Abruptly George set down his fork and stared at his plate, his face flushed.

Private Mackenzie leaned over to Hattie. "That one surely has a knack for making folks feel special."

Hattie nodded. "She surely does."

December 1864

20.

A BRIGHT FIRE CRACKLED in the parlor one evening in early December as Teddy sprawled in front of the hearth, surrounded by tin soldiers battling across the woolen carpet. Hattie perched on a footstool nearby, idly flipping through an old *Harper's* magazine. Miss Taft sat knitting a pair of red mittens for a young relative out East, and Father and Mr. Jenkins were reading newspapers.

Hattie studied an illustration of Santa Claus, clad in striped pants and a star-studded jacket, delivering gifts to the Union troops. "Father, I'm glad you're here in Milwaukee instead of away in the army like George's father."

Father grunted behind his paper.

Teddy looked up from his armies. "Do you reckon the Rebel children will have Christmas?"

Miss Taft lowered her needles abruptly. "Why, of course they will! What makes you say such a thing?"

Teddy said confidently, "The naval blockade keeps supplies from getting through to the Confederates. Isn't that right, Mister Jenkins?"

"What's that, Teddy?"

Her eyes on the half-finished mitten, Miss Taft replied sharply, "That may be, but the children in the Confederate states will certainly celebrate Christmas."

Mr. Jenkins glanced at her and nodded. "Miss Taft is right, of course."

"I wouldn't want them to be cold or hungry," Hattie said, "even if they are Rebels."

"I'm glad to hear that," said Miss Taft, but she sounded strangely sad. Not glad at all.

Mother entered the parlor with a taffeta dress and black shawl draped over her arm. "Hattie and Teddy, the Society has begun a Christmas collection for soldiers' families. What can you two give to the children?"

"They're not getting my armies." Teddy spread his arms over the tin soldiers.

"Very well, dear. Put those away and run upstairs to find other things to give."

Hattie considered. "If I give away my dolls and their clothes, might I have a base-ball bat for Christmas? Teddy left the old bat out in the rain."

"I did not! George was supposed to put it away."

Miss Taft looked up from her knitting. "A bat hardly seems like an appropriate gift for a young lady."

"I think it seems like a perfect gift," said Hattie. "Don't you, Father?"

"What's that, Hattie girl?"

"Wouldn't a base-ball bat be a fine gift?"

"Yes, a fine gift."

"Father, you're not even listening! I would like to have my own bat."

Mother tapped her foot impatiently. "Hattie, you may donate your outgrown dresses and shoes. And I know you both have books and toys you haven't touched in years. Let's give them to a poor child whose father is away at war."

Hattie knelt on the carpet to help Teddy put the soldiers into their chipboard box. "If we don't choose our own donations," she murmured, "Mother will choose them for us."

On Christmas morning Hattie woke to Teddy's voice across their attic bedroom. She pulled the quilts over her cold nose and mumbled, "I wish Ellen were here to start a fire. It's freezing."

"George has to start the fires at his house all the time." Teddy had already put on his robe and slippers. He knelt on the trunk and scratched at the frost on the window pane. "It's snowing again," he said. "A perfect Christmas day."

Hattie reached for her stockings, burrowing underneath the blankets to pull them over her icy feet. Gritting her teeth, she threw back her blankets, pulled on her robe and slippers, and scurried across the attic to thump downstairs after Teddy.

"Merry Christmas!" Mother called from her sitting room. "Come and warm up in here. Your father is lighting the fire down in the parlor."

Hattie pulled Mother's embroidered footstool close to

the little stove, holding her cold hands toward the flames.

Teddy plopped on the rug beside her, pulling his robe tightly around him.

When Father called them downstairs, the fire had not yet taken the chill out of the parlor. In the corner of the room stood the Christmas tree glistening with gilded walnuts, tri-colored ribbons, and tin stars. As Teddy admired the lighted candles in the branches, Hattie smiled to see a long slender package underneath the tree.

Teddy grinned as he found a little round package with his name on it. He tugged at the red ribbon and tore off the paper. "Look at this, Hattie—it's a regulation base ball from New York!"

"Now close your eyes, Hattie," said Mother. "This one was too pretty to wrap." Hattie opened her eyes to see a little green workbasket embroidered with flowers. She lifted the lid to find brightly colored skeins of worsted yarn. Running her fingers over the soft wool, Hattie said, "This is so beautiful. It doesn't seem to be suitable for knitting socks for soldiers."

"What else is in that workbasket?"

Hattie discovered side pockets with needles and a scissors, a roll of wire, and a folded sheet of paper. She unfolded instructions for making flowers from worsted and wire.

"Anything else in there?" asked Father.

Hattie pulled out a pack of playing cards tied with yarn. She untied the bow and fanned out the cards. "Look, Teddy! The four suits are stars, shields, eagles, and flags. There's a Goddess of Liberty for the queen."

She set aside the workbasket. "Teddy, what else is under the tree?"

Teddy reached for the long package, but instead of handing it to Hattie, he began to untie the ribbon.

"Teddy, what are you doing?"

"It has my name on it—see?"

The wrapping fell away to a reveal a wooden bat gleaming in the firelight. "It's a beauty," Teddy whispered.

Hattie stared in disbelief. "But *I* asked for a bat."

"I'm sure your brother will let you play sometimes," said Father. "Won't you, Teddy boy?"

"*Let* me play?"

"A base-ball bat is no gift for a young lady," Mother said crisply.

Hattie stood up, scattering stars and eagles, shields and flags all over the carpet. "Then I don't want to be a young lady! It just isn't *fair*."

21.

WHEN TEDDY CAME DOWNSTAIRS the next morning, Mother was sticking cloves into an enormous ham while Hattie chopped onions for the charity dinners for soldiers' families.

"I can't wait to show George my new bat and ball. Maybe we'll get up a game today."

Mother smiled. "Perhaps you should wait until spring."

"This is the perfect time," said Teddy. "The garden's covered with snow so we can have our field again."

Hattie ignored Teddy and blinked back stinging tears. At the sound of knocking she set down the knife, swiped her face with the hem of her pinafore, and rinsed her hands before going to the back door. There on the porch stood Charlie Moores.

"Merry Christmas, Hattie!" He looked at her face. "You don't look very merry."

"I've been chopping onions."

"Charlie!" called Teddy. "Let me show you my new bat and ball." He fetched his bat from beneath the bench and pulled the ball from his pocket.

"That's a fine one," said Charlie, running his thumb over the stitching. "These are not easy to make."

Hattie glared at Teddy as he held up the new bat for Charlie to admire.

"Don't stand with the door open," Mother called from the kitchen. "Invite him in."

"I can't stay," said Charlie. "I came to say that I'm getting up a sleighing party on Friday. We're to ride out to my uncle's farm and have popcorn and a taffy pull." He held out a little envelope. "Ma wrote out an invitation. I hope you two can come. Now I'd best get these delivered. I'll see you Friday!"

Hattie hurried back to the kitchen. "May we go?"

Mother looked up from the cranberries simmering on the stove. "Your father will be up in St. Paul, and Ellen won't return till Saturday. I could have a quiet evening at home. Hattie, you may write to say that you and Teddy would be delighted to attend."

Later that afternoon Hattie and Mother waited on the front porch for the Buttricks to arrive. Teddy had gone sledding, and Mother left a cold supper for him and Father in the kitchen.

While Colonel Buttrick loaded their heavy baskets into the sleigh, Mrs. Buttrick greeted them warmly. "How wonderful to have another pair of willing hands. I've just been told that several of our members must stay home because their children are ill."

After the sleigh pulled up in front of the Soldiers' Home, the colonel helped carry the baskets inside. Mrs. Hewitt assigned Hattie to a table of sweets in the kitchen and showed her how to cut and wrap the gingerbread. A package of gingerbread and three oranges were to be tucked into each boxed dinner for distribution to the families waiting outside.

Hattie worked steadily, hardly looking up, transforming the fragrant gingerbread into neat little packages. The moment she finished packing a box, a soldier carried it to the front door. Hattie did not know how much time had passed when she noticed that the orange crates were almost empty.

Mrs. Vedder, who stood at the door handing out boxes to a line of women and children, called, "Oh dear. Lydia, Fanny—come here, please."

The three women met in the front room for a quick conference, and then Mrs. Hewitt returned and tapped a serving spoon against a roasting pan, silencing the voices in the kitchen.

"My dear friends, it seems that we have grossly underestimated the number of soldiers' families in need. As you see, we are nearly out of dinners, and there is still a long line waiting outside. Missus Buttrick and Missus Vedder and I have determined that we must offer another dinner on Friday for those who must do without tonight."

Friday—Hattie stared at Mother in horror.

After breakfast on Friday morning, Hattie worked without complaint in the kitchen. Although Mother had assured her that she and Teddy could attend the sleighing party, Hattie was still half-afraid that she would change her mind. But Teddy dawdled at his tasks until Hattie hissed, "Nothing will keep *you* from the sleighing party, but if we don't finish, Mother will keep me home to help.

Don't you understand anything?"

By mid-afternoon even Mother was frustrated with Teddy. At last she said, "If you can't move any faster than that, you might as well go up to bed!"

Teddy stood up, swaying slightly, and murmured, "Yes, ma'am." His cheeks were bright red and beads of sweat stood on his upper lip.

"Why, Teddy—" Mother laid the back of her hand across his forehead. "You're burning up! I'm so sorry—" Within moments she had whisked him off to the daybed in her sitting room. Returning to the kitchen for a basin and cloth, she murmured, "That poor boy. I should have seen he was ill, but I kept thinking about the soldiers' families—" Her voice trembled, and Hattie looked up in astonishment to see Mother blinking back tears. "Sometimes I don't think enough about my own family."

Hattie felt her eyes watering. "Yes, you do," she said, her throat so tight she could hardly speak.

Mother wiped her cheeks with the corner of the cloth. "Tonight I shall stay home and look after my own child." She picked up the basin. "You must go to the Soldiers' Home in my place."

"But tonight is the sleighing party!"

Mother's eyes flashed. "Think of those poor women and children standing in the cold."

"But it's not fair!" Tears of anger stung Hattie's eyes. "You said I could go—I've worked hard all day."

"Other women have been working hard, too—we mustn't shirk our responsibility to them."

"I'm not shirking! I'm just so tired of doing everything

to help the soldiers. When is this war ever going to *end*? I might never have another chance to go to a sleighing party with Charlie!"

"Don't be silly," Mother said. "You have a lifetime of opportunities ahead."

A few hours later Hattie stood waiting on the porch while two sleighs passed one another on the street, the passengers hailing one another merrily over the jingling of the bells. When the Buttrick sleigh pulled up to the Bigelow house, she made her way through the softly falling snow to climb in beside Mrs. Buttrick while the driver loaded the baskets.

"Why, Hattie, I didn't expect to see you tonight," said Mrs. Buttrick. "I thought you were going to a—" she broke off abruptly.

Keeping her eyes on the falling snow, Hattie said, "Mother sends her regrets. Teddy's not well. I've come in her place."

The driver picked up the reins, and the sleigh lurched forward with a jingling of bells.

When they arrived at the Home, Mrs. Buttrick slipped on an apron and took command of the volunteers, assigning them each a task. "Your mother was going to hand out boxes, Hattie, and you could do that just as well. Please wish each of the families a blessed Christmas on our behalf."

Wrapping herself in a warm woolen shawl, Hattie took her place at the front door. A number of neatly packed boxes were already in place. At five o'clock Hattie sighed, opened the door, and began handing out the dinners.

"Merry Christmas, ma'am," she said dutifully to the first woman in line.

She was startled to see tears glisten in the woman's eyes as she whispered, "Bless you, miss."

Some time later, Hattie was tired of standing and thankful that the boxes were almost gone.

"Merry Christmas, ma'am." Suddenly she found herself staring at George's mother. "Why, Missus Sch . . ." she said in surprise, stopping when she saw her neighbor's face turn red.

Hattie began again. "A blessed Christmas to you, ma'am, from all of us at the Soldiers' Home Society."

"Thank you, miss," murmured Mrs. Schaefer as she took the box from Hattie.

As Mrs. Schaefer vanished into the night, Hattie thought of George scrambling for old vegetables in the garden. She squared her shoulders and smiled as she handed out the last few boxes. "A blessed Christmas to you, ma'am."

January 1865

22.

O N NEW YEAR'S DAY Hattie sat at the parlor table
with a rainbow of worsted spread before her. A wire
wrapped in green yarn formed a lopsided leaf, but the
purple yarn wrapped around loops of wire did not look
anything like a violet.

Outside, the usually quiet street bustled with men
paying New Year's calls. Father and Mr. Jenkins had gone
out to make the traditional visits to neighbors and friends.

Hattie heard footsteps on the front porch and the
sharp rap of the door knocker. Some acquaintance must
not know that Mother was not receiving today because of
Teddy's illness. Hattie went to the door, preparing polite
words to send the caller away.

Charlie Moores stood on the front porch. "Happy New
Year, Hattie. Sorry you had to miss the sleighing party. I
brought you and Teddy some taffy." He held out a small
package.

Before Hattie could respond, Ellen spoke from behind
her. "Have you forgotten your manners entirely, darlin'?

Wish your caller a happy New Year and invite him into the parlor. Haven't I baked for all of these hours, and nobody here but you?" She bustled off to the kitchen.

Charlie chuckled. "Dear Ellen."

Hattie watched him hang up his coat and cap—how odd to see him at the front door instead of the back—and led him into the parlor. They sat on either side of the table, and Charlie picked up the little bent-wire flower among the tangled yarn.

"It's supposed to be a violet. I don't seem to have the knack for this sort of thing." She opened the lid of the workbasket and swept the pile of worsted off the table.

Charlie set down the flower. "You'll get better with practice. It's the same with anything, isn't it? Drumming or base ball or—"

"I'd rather practice base ball."

Ellen carried a tray into the parlor. "Here you are, my dears."

Charlie heaped his plate with shortbread and ginger-bread and teacakes. "Teddy will be sorry he missed this. Mind you save him some taffy."

"I'd like to play cards or something else to amuse him, but Mother won't let me near."

Charlie nodded, swallowing. "She's right to keep you away. Remember the fever in Memphis?"

Hattie cradled the teacup in her hand. "When you were in Memphis, did any of the soldiers worry about their families back home?"

"What do you mean?"

"Did they wonder whether their wives had enough

money to feed the children?"

Charlie took another piece of gingerbread. "I made sure Mother received all of my pay. But I heard some of the long-timers talk about how their pay didn't always make it home. Why do you ask?"

Hattie sipped her tea. "So many women stood in line for those Christmas dinners. It's not fair that families should suffer when soldiers are away from home."

Charlie reached for more shortbread. "Why don't those women write to their husbands and tell them they need more money?"

Hattie remembered Mrs. Schaefer's red face at the Soldiers' Home that evening. She set down her teacup. "Charlie, some people just prefer to bear their burdens alone."

The front door opened, sending a draft of cold air from the hall. A few moments later, Mr. Jenkins entered the parlor. "Happy New Year, Charlie! Hattie, you are quite the young lady, receiving callers this year."

Hattie felt her cheeks grow warm. She had barely spoken to Mr. Jenkins since his return from the holiday visit to relatives out East.

Charlie stood to shake hands with Mr. Jenkins. "Hattie's a fine hostess, but I'm not a good guest," he said. "I've eaten everything and left nothing for you."

Mr. Jenkins patted his vest. "I've made plenty of calls today." He looked directly at Hattie. "May I join you?"

She managed a smile. "Please do."

Charlie sat back down, and Mr. Jenkins pulled a chair closer to the table. "I've been meaning to talk to you,

Hattie. The New Year is a time for new beginnings, don't you think?"

Hattie looked into his eyes, then looked away. "Yes, sir."

"Suppose you attended a base-ball game and cheered for Charlie's side, but Missus Buttrick was cheering for the other side. Would she no longer be your friend?"

Hattie stared at him. "Of course not. We both love base ball."

"Exactly. Opponents need not be enemies. You and I both love our country, and we both want the war to end. We're just cheering for different sides in the same game." He reached into his vest pocket. "I have a New Year's gift for you." He held out a small yellow booklet.

"For me?" In wonder Hattie took the booklet, read the cover—*1865 Beadle's Dime Base-Ball Player*—and flipped open the pages of rules and guidelines. "Thank you, Mister Jenkins!"

He smiled. "I bought that in New York over Christmas and read it on the train west. Mind you, I may need to borrow your official guide this spring to review the rules."

Charlie sat up straighter. "Are you starting up the Milwaukee Base Ball Club again?"

Mr. Jenkins' smile disappeared. "Not till this war is over, Charlie. Not till then."

23.

A WEEK LATER, HATTIE WAITED with the tea cart in the chilly hall, which smelled of damp wool from the women's wraps on the coat tree outside the parlor. She heard the voice of Mrs. Hewitt announcing that the war department had authorized government rations for the soldiers. "According to the report, a regular allowance will be issued to the Home forthwith."

"Forthwith? When has the government ever done anything 'forthwith'?" The sharp voice belonged to Mrs. Eisenmenger. "I daresay we'll still be waiting for those provisions while trainloads of crippled soldiers pull into Milwaukee and we haven't beds enough for them all."

"That is precisely why we must renovate the building." Mrs. Hewitt sounded impatient. "According to my measurements, twenty extra feet of frontage will provide space for two dozen beds."

"Yes, yet another fundraiser," countered Mrs. Eisenmenger. "Another Washington's Birthday Gala, another spring bazaar. A strawberry festival, a summer sociable, and another harvest fair. When will it ever *end*?" Her voice was shrill. "I'm so *tired* of doing all this work for the soldiers. I ask you, how many more years must we be expected to carry on?"

Hattie cringed at the echo of her own words to Mother

in the kitchen that December night.

For a long stretch of time the only sound in the parlor was the ticking of the mantel clock.

Then Mrs. Buttrick spoke. "I, for one, will continue to work for our boys as long I have breath in my body."

Tears prickled Hattie's eyes at the passion in that voice.

"As will I," said Mrs. Hewitt.

"And I." That was Mrs. Vedder.

Without thinking further, Hattie stepped through the doorway. "And I!"

For a moment the startled members of the Soldiers' Home Society stared at her. Then Mrs. Buttrick's delighted laugh rippled through the room. "Hattie Bigelow, that's exactly the spirit we need."

"Madame President and members of the Society—" Mother's voice was brisk. "I recommend that we pause for refreshment."

Hattie rolled the tea cart into the parlor, and Mother began pouring tea, clearly not as pleased as Mrs. Buttrick had been by Hattie's remark.

Silently and skillfully, Hattie delivered the cups around. While the other women chatted about their children or their needlework, Mrs. Buttrick, Mrs. Hewitt, and Mrs. Vedder continued to discuss the business of the Society.

"Whether the war ends in a month or in a year," said Mrs. Hewitt "we *must* make plans for a permanent home. We have outgrown our rented rooms. It's high time we begin raising money for a real Soldiers' Home, designed to our patients' needs."

Mrs. Buttrick nodded. "We ought to look at property outside the city. So many of our Wisconsin boys feel trapped in town—they need woods and fields, and acreage for gardens and livestock to grow as much of their own food as possible."

"I picture a fine new brick building," added Mrs. Vedder, "with a big kitchen and a huge dining hall."

Hattie tried to imagine a brick building out in the rolling hills where she and her classmates had gone berry picking last summer.

"The Great Northwestern Fair will rob us of donations from our south counties," fretted Mrs. Hewitt. "I do wish we didn't have competition from Chicago."

Hattie offered a silver plate of teacakes to the three women.

Mrs. Buttrick took one and thanked her, then added lightly, "Hattie, what would you do if you were in charge of raising money for a new Soldiers' Home?"

"I wouldn't let Chicago stop me," Hattie said promptly. "If I were in charge, I'd plan a fair in Milwaukee just as big as Chicago's, and I'd tell everybody in Wisconsin to support our fair instead of theirs."

Mrs. Vedder blinked. "That sounds a bit uncharitable."

Hattie reddened, but answered firmly, "Opponents need not be enemies. Milwaukee and Chicago are just cheering for different sides in the same game."

"Hattie Bigelow!" Mother's voice was stern. "Some of our guests are still waiting for their refreshments."

"Yes, ma'am." Hattie left the three women in the corner and returned to her place at the cart.

As the Bigelow household sat in the parlor after dinner a week later, Mother and Miss Taft were knitting, and Hattie and Teddy sat near the fireplace playing cards, the bright pasteboard stars, shields, eagles, and flags spread on the carpet between them. Father read *Harper's Weekly,* while Mr. Jenkins read the newspaper. With a sudden rustling of the pages, Mr. Jenkins said, "Now here's something of local interest." Clearing his throat, he read aloud:

"A meeting has been called for at the Chamber of Commerce, to make arrangements for a State Fair for the benefit of the Soldiers' Home in this city. A general attendance of ladies and gentlemen is invited. The hour is two o'clock."

Father looked up from his *Harper's*. "I thought Chicago was to hold a big fair this summer."

"Yes, but ours will be different," Hattie explained. "Our fair is going to raise enough money to buy land in the country and build a new Soldiers' Home!"

Father chuckled and opened his magazine again. "The ladies of Milwaukee certainly have some grand plans."

February 1865

24.

ONE SNOWY EVENING as the Bigelows and their boarders sat down to dinner, Mother could hardly wait to share the news. "The state legislature has approved our proposal to build a permanent Soldiers' Home *and* has authorized a Fair to begin on June twenty-eighth."

Hattie ticked off the months on her fingers. "It's less than five months away!"

"That's a tremendous amount of work—and money for expenses," said Father. "How do you ladies expect to manage?"

Mother smiled. "We're canvassing the city and asking everyone to give just one day's wages—or one day's profit—to support the Fair. We began with City Hall."

Teddy turned to Mr. Jenkins. "Did you give your share?"

Father frowned. "Teddy boy, that's not the sort of thing one gentleman asks another."

Hattie set down her fork. "But if nobody talks about it, how will people know they ought to give?"

Mr. Jenkins raised his glass. "I am pleased to report that I have pledged my share."

"What about you, Father?" said Teddy. "How do you calculate a day's profit? The shop makes plenty of money every time the army puts in another order for boots and brogans."

Hattie stared at Father. "Isn't taking money from the army exactly the wrong thing for us to do?"

"Hattie Bigelow!" said Mother. "That is quite enough."

Father sat back in his chair. "Hattie girl, I do sell to the army. I sell quality goods. My brogans are stitched, not pegged—no chance of them falling apart after the first march. And you may be sure that Bigelow and Company will contribute generously to the Soldiers' Home Fair."

In the silence that followed, Miss Taft said, "The sixth grade girls have chosen to sew a doll's wardrobe to auction at the February gala. Each girl is to sew a set of items for a particular season."

"How lovely," said Mother. "Hattie, what do you intend to sew?"

"I don't believe I'll be sewing at all."

"But you have a beautiful new workbasket and all the supplies."

Hattie nodded. "Yes, I do. Teddy and I are going to sell worsted flowers as our one day's effort."

Teddy gaped at her, fork in midair.

On Saturday Hattie stood in the kitchen with a basket full of brightly colored yarn flowers while Teddy watched Ellen mixing cake batter. "Teddy, you will help me, won't you? If I don't sell flowers, I'll have to sew doll clothes with Lizzie."

"What's wrong with that?" Teddy asked as Ellen handed him the wooden spoon.

Hattie stamped her foot. "I will not take orders from Lizzie Eisenmenger!" She lowered her voice. "I'll let you have my *Beadle's Base-Ball* guide for a whole day."

Teddy licked his spoon. "How about a whole week?"

Hattie sighed. "Yes, a whole week. Now, we'll begin selling in front of Father's shop. Mrs. Buttrick gave me some circulars about the one day's effort as well."

While Teddy fetched his coat, Hattie took an empty half-pint jar from the pantry.

Ellen pulled two cents from the pocket of her apron. "'Tis bad luck to set out on a journey empty-handed. Here's a little something to sweeten the pot."

As Hattie and Teddy crossed the bridge, a bitter wind blew along the river. Hattie hunched her shoulders inside her coat as Teddy calculated. "If we sell 'em for a penny each, we'll earn twenty-five cents. That's respectable for one day's effort, don't you think?"

"I suppose so," said Hattie. "But it took me more than one day to make them all."

Outside the boot and shoe shop, Teddy walked up to an elderly couple and said, "My name is Teddy Bigelow. My father owns this shop, and my mother is a manager of the Soldiers' Home. My sister made these flowers to support the Soldiers' Home Fair. How many would you like to buy?"

The gentleman dropped a penny in the jar while his wife chose a pink rose from the basket. The coins rattled in the jar as the children continued to approach passers-by, many of whom avoided them.

Hattie's fingers felt numb inside her gloves. "I'm cold, Teddy. Let's go inside."

"They're your flowers. Do whatever you please," he replied. "I'm going to ask Father if I can help in the shop."

The tin bell jingled as the children entered the shop. Charlie glanced toward them, then turned back to his customer.

"Father, may I sell my flowers in here?"

He shook his head. "We sell boots and shoes."

"May I give them away?"

"As long as you don't disturb my customers. Teddy, see what you can do to straighten up. We've had a very good morning."

When Father brought a customer to the cash drawer to finish the sale, Hattie pulled a yellow daisy from her basket. "Good morning, sir. Please take this flower to remember our brave soldiers."

"I'm sorry. I don't care to buy flowers."

"This is a gift," Hattie said firmly. "Please take it to remember our soldiers."

The gentleman smiled and accepted the daisy. "Why, thank you." When Father handed him his change, he dropped two cents in the jar tucked inside the basket.

As Hattie waited for another customer, she watched Charlie.

"These Congress gaiters are a popular choice," he said.

He pointed out the rugged stitching on the soles, praised the suppleness of the leather, and stretched the elastic gussets on the side. "Nice and easy to slip on and off."

When Charlie carried the gaiters to the cash drawer, Hattie said to the buyer, "Please take a flower to remember our soldiers."

"Thank you, miss."

After Charlie finished the sale, Hattie pulled a circular from her basket. "I surely hope you will donate a day's wages to the Soldiers' Home Fair. Everyone must do his part."

Charlie snatched the flyer away from her. "I'm sorry sir," he said, glaring at Hattie. "She doesn't understand how a business operates."

The man nodded curtly and hurried out the door.

"Don't try that again," warned Charlie, his voice colder than she had ever heard before.

Her face burning, Hattie turned away and set her basket on Father's desk. She sat in his chair and stared sullenly at the columns in his ledger.

As he walked past the desk, she called, "Father, you made forty-five dollars yesterday. Is that what you're going to donate to the Fair?"

Father's mouth opened. Abruptly he slammed the ledger shut and handed her the flower basket. "We'll discuss this at home, Hattie girl."

"And now how did you fare?" Ellen asked when Hattie entered the warm kitchen. She glanced at the jar in the basket. "I see more coins and fewer flowers. That seems a

110

good day's effort."

Hattie shrugged.

Ellen eyed her and said gently, "Fetch me up some vegetables for a fine beef stew."

Holding a lantern and a basket, Hattie clomped down into the cellar. Some of the bushels and pecks that had been heaping at harvest time were empty now. As Hattie reached into a bushel of potatoes, she felt a soft one among them.

She began rooting through all the bushels, searching for spoilage. When she returned to the kitchen with Ellen's vegetables, she brought half a sack of spoiled ones, too.

Setting down Ellen's basket, Hattie wrapped herself in a shawl and carried the sack out into the twilight, slipping through the bare hedge to the Schaefers' yard. She knocked on the back door of the house.

Mrs. Schaefer opened the door, holding a toddler on her hip. She did not invite Hattie inside.

Hattie held up the sack. "I was down in the root cellar, and I saw that some of the vegetables have bad spots. But there's still plenty of good, too, so I thought perhaps you could use them . . ."

"I'm sure Ellen can cut out the bad parts." Mrs. Schaefer made no move to take the sack.

Hattie said quickly, "But Ellen's eyesight isn't what it used to be, and she frets so that we don't want her to bother with such things." Hattie hoped that Ellen would forgive her lies.

From behind his mother, George said, "I could cut out the bad spots."

"I can't keep these in the cellar, and I don't want to spoil the rest of the harvest." Hattie thrust the sack at George.

Mrs. Schaefer's lips twitched into a smile. "Thank you, Hattie. We will be glad to help you out."

Hattie pulled her shawl tighter as she crossed the snow-covered garden and tried to calculate how much more ground she ought to break in the spring. At the back porch she remembered that she would be in trouble when Father came home. Still, glancing back at the light in the Schaefers' kitchen, she was content with her day's effort.

March 1865

25.

"PLEASE BE SEATED," Miss Taft said to the class. "This morning we will listen to our President's Inaugural Address." She picked up a folded newspaper and began to read aloud. Hattie settled into her seat, imagining the gray and drizzling day on which President Lincoln stood to address the crowds in front of the newly finished capitol dome in Washington.

As Miss Taft read the speech, Lizzie Eisenmenger whispered to a friend, and two boys scuffled at their desks in the back corner. Perhaps their fathers had supported General McClellan. Hattie gave her full attention to Miss Taft, so that none of her classmates would have any doubt about whom *she* had supported.

"With malice toward none, with charity for all, with firmness in the right as God gives us to see the right, let us strive on to finish the work we are in,—"

Miss Taft paused, and when she spoke again her voice trembled.

"—*to bind up the nation's wounds, to care for him who shall have borne the battle and for his widow and his orphan,*—"

Again she paused, and Hattie saw tears glistening on her cheeks.

"—*to do all which may achieve and cherish a just and lasting peace among ourselves and with all nations.*"

In the silence that followed, Miss Taft laid the newspaper on her desk and turned away from the students, head bowed and handkerchief in hand. Hattie began clapping so hard that most of her classmates joined in.

When Miss Taft faced the class again, she said gently, "Children, the burden of binding up the nation's wounds will be borne by your generation for many years to come. We must all do our part in helping to care for our soldiers and their families, beginning with our efforts to support the Soldiers' Home Fair."

Lizzie stood up. "Yes, Miss Taft. My sewing society raised forty dollars at the Washington's Birthday Gala." She looked pointedly at Hattie. "Those of us who sewed doll clothes are certainly doing our part."

Hattie lifted her chin. "Lizzie Eisenmenger, my garden fed the soldiers for months and months!"

"Girls!" Miss Taft's eyes were on Hattie. "I am disappointed in you. This is *not* a time for quarreling. Please turn to today's arithmetic lesson."

Hattie slumped in her seat and pulled out her book and slate.

When she and Teddy arrived home after school, Hattie paused at the gate to look at the garden, a frozen sea of mud with islands of melting snow. Inside, the house was warm and fragrant with the smell of baking bread. Hattie studied the row of golden-brown loaves on the kitchen table. "You've certainly baked plenty of bread this week."

"That I have," said Ellen, nodding her head. "Sure, and I hardly know what I was thinking."

"We could take some to the Soldiers' Home," said Teddy.

Hattie shook her head. "No, the bakeries donate enough bread." She added slowly, "Ellen, perhaps you could send a couple of loaves to the Schaefers. You know how much George likes your baking."

"If they're going to George, I'll take them," said Teddy. "He's *my* friend."

As Ellen wrapped two loaves in a dish towel, Hattie took a jar of blackberry preserves from the pantry. Teddy slid the jar into his pocket and picked up the bread.

"Mind you don't stay too long," Ellen said as she opened the door for him, smiling at Hattie behind his back.

Hattie sighed. "You're surely doing your part to support the cause, Ellen. I must see Missus Buttrick about doing mine."

When she entered the back door of the Soldiers' Home, she found Mrs. Buttrick unpacking a crate of donations.

Without any greeting Hattie burst out in a flurry of words. "Missus Buttrick, I need to know how I can do my part to bind the nation's wounds. I just can't *bear* to join Liz—to join the girls' sewing society, but I do want to help. I want to do important work at the Home and at the Soldiers' Home Fair and—and *everywhere.*"

Mrs. Buttrick smiled. "I appreciate your zeal, Hattie. You may begin by putting away these jars."

"That's not exactly what I meant." But Hattie dutifully carried the pickles and beets to the pantry. Returning for another load, she said, "Father talks as if women don't understand how to run a business, but managing the Soldiers' Home is like running a business, isn't it?"

Mrs. Buttrick nodded. "And the Soldiers' Home Fair is an enormous undertaking in itself. Next week I will spend several days visiting soldiers' aid societies in Racine County. I intend to remind the ladies that Milwaukee and Chicago need not be enemies, for all of us are playing in the same game."

"I wish I could travel to raise money. What more can *I* do?"

Mrs. Buttrick considered. "That garden of yours is a godsend to us, Hattie. Please plant lettuces and peas as early as you can. The sooner we can serve fresh greens to our boys, the healthier they will be."

Hattie squared her shoulders. "Yes, *ma'am.*"

26.

O N A COLD GRAY AFTERNOON a week later, Hattie and
Teddy stood in the yard inspecting the garden plot.
Teddy shivered. "It's still frozen. There's no point in think-
ing about planting now."

"We're *planning*, not planting."

He stuck his hands into his coat pockets. "I reckon we
could plan just as well inside."

Hattie pulled up one of the old pickets from the end
of a row. "This year we'll break more ground on this side
and—"

"*More* ground?"

Hattie brandished her picket like a sword. "Yes, we
need longer rows to increase our yield." With the point of
the picket she traced a line in the mud as she walked the
length of the garden. "We'll leave a path down the middle
wide enough for the wagon."

Rat-a-tat-a-tat!

Hattie turned to see Charlie Moores grinning over the
fence, drumsticks in hand.

She pointed toward the garden with her picket. "This
year a garden path will go from home base to the pitcher's
mound. So you'll be able to bat from the old home plate.
Just like old times!"

"That should save a window or two." He beat another quick tattoo on the fence.

Teddy eyed Charlie. "Why do you have your drumsticks?"

"Can you guess?"

Teddy grinned. "You've re-enlisted!"

Hattie dropped the picket. "Oh no, Charlie. You haven't, have you?"

"You are looking at a musician of the Forty-eighth Wisconsin Infantry."

"But the war's almost over. Why do they need more troops?"

"You don't sound very patriotic," said Teddy. "You should be proud of Charlie."

Hattie glared at him, then turned to Charlie. "What about base ball? Mister Jenkins is going to start up the club again, remember? And why can't you support the cause right here in Milwaukee? You could help us—we're planting a bigger garden."

"Base ball will wait. The war won't. You inspired me, Hattie. All that talk of one day's effort convinced me that I am worth more as a soldier than as a shop boy."

Stricken, Hattie glanced into his blue eyes and then looked away, hunching her shoulders and putting her cold hands into her coat pockets. Her fingers touched something, and she pulled out a worsted purple daisy. Smiling bravely, she held out the crumpled flower. "It's bad luck to say farewell empty-handed."

Charlie twirled the flower in his fingers. "In the language of flowers, what does this mean?"

"Just farewell."

He tucked the stem of the purple flower into his belt next to his drumsticks. "I leave for camp the day after tomorrow. I reckon I'll be home before the daisies bloom."

Hattie shivered. She could no longer imagine anything blooming.

Charlie clapped Teddy on the shoulder. "You keep the neighborhood boys in line."

Teddy saluted him. "Yes, sir!"

"Hattie, I know you'll look after my sisters." As snowflakes began to fall from the leaden sky, he leaned over the fence to kiss her on the forehead. "Don't worry about me. Farewell." Turning jauntily on his heel, he marched away in the falling snow.

Hattie leaned on the fence and watched until he disappeared around the corner.

On the back porch she and Teddy stomped their feet and brushed the snow from one another's shoulders. When Teddy ducked into the kitchen, Hattie ran up the stairs. In the dim bedroom on the third floor, she sank down beside the trunk and peered out the window at the Moores' house. As the cold dark enveloped her, she laid her head in her arms and sobbed for Charlie, marching forth to war.

April 1865

27.

A T SCHOOL ONE MONDAY MORNING a few weeks later, while her classmates worked arithmetic problems, Hattie sketched her garden, plotting rows of lettuce and carrots and peas.

Boom!

Hattie dropped her chalk as the classroom windows rattled.

Boom!

Several girls squealed, and the students looked at one another in confusion. Hattie was first out of her seat— "Those are cannons firing!"—and first to open a window. A puff of smoke rose near the river.

Boom!

As the boys jostled one another at the windows, excited voices rose from the street below. *"Lee surrenders! War ends!"*

"The war is over!" Hattie and the boys exulted to the clanging of the bells of St. Gall's.

Something inside her exploded like a firework—Charlie would come home and Mr. Jenkins would start up the base-ball club again. Snatching the flag from its holder, she held it aloft and cried "The Union forever!"

"Rally 'round the flag, boys!" shouted somebody else. Boys and girls together began clapping and marching in time to the song:

> *"Our country forever,*
> *Hurrah, boys, hurrah!*
> *Down with the traitor—"*

"Enough!" Miss Taft's sharp voice cut through the singing. "Return to your seats at once. Hattie Bigelow, put that flag where it belongs."

The other students scrambled back to their desks, and Hattie was left alone at the front of the room. The classroom door opened and Principal Martin announced that school was dismissed. More cheering erupted from the students, and Miss Taft retreated in apparent surrender.

"Here, girls," she said faintly, holding up the sewing circle's basket of tri-colored rosettes. "Take enough for your families." She sat stiffly at her desk, her hands folded in front of her.

Hattie grabbed several rosettes and squeezed through the crowded cloakroom to get her coat and gallop down the stairs.

She met Teddy and George in the schoolyard with the Moores girls. Other church bells were ringing now, near and far.

Bea clutched Hattie's arm. "Why are we going home? Is the war here?"

Hattie took her hand. "No, Bea—we're celebrating. The war is over."

Molly seized Bea's other hand. "And Charlie's coming home!"

"My pa, too," said George. "I want to be first to tell my ma." He charged away down the sidewalk.

Bea shook her hand free from Hattie's. "I want to be first to tell our mama!"

"No, wait for me!" cried Molly, and the two clattered away after George.

Hattie looked at Teddy. "Our mother was probably the first to know—let's go to meet her at the Soldiers' Home."

When Hattie and Teddy burst through the front door of the Soldiers' Home, they nearly ran into two soldiers, who were draped with yards of red, white and blue bunting. Mother greeted them with a startled "Children, why aren't you in school?"

Teddy waved his cap. "No school 'cause there's no more war!"

A hearty cheer went up from the soldiers in the sitting room.

As Hattie pinned a rosette to her bodice, Mother asked her and Teddy to help in decorating the porch. "None of the men will rest until we've hung the bunting, and some of them really must. Then go to see your father at the shop."

Outside, Hattie and Private Mackenzie untangled the red, white and blue yardage. Another soldier lifted Teddy onto his shoulders to tie the bunting to the eaves. "Charlie and his regiment must be celebrating, too," Teddy said as he fastened another festoon.

Hattie draped bunting over the rail. "I wish he were celebrating here."

An impromptu kitchen band paraded up the street, and the soldiers on the porch stomped in time to the banging of pots and pans and began to sing, *"Glory, glory, hallelujah! Glory, glory, hallelujah!"*

Hattie and Teddy followed the band across the bridge to East Water Street, where almost every building was festooned in red, white and blue. Swaths of bunting hung from second-story windows and porches, and shop doors bloomed with tricolored wreaths. In the front window of the Bigelow shop, the Stars and Stripes sprouted out of every boot and brogan.

"Father!" called Teddy as the shop bell jingled. "Did you save a flag for me?"

Father held out his arms and pulled the children into a great bear hug. After Hattie pinned her last rosette on his lapel, he handed them each a small flag, put on his hat, and flipped the "CLOSED" sign under the ribbons on the front door.

The streets were bustling with exuberant Milwaukeeans of all ages as schoolchildren mingled with store owners and patrons. A carriage of local officials led a hastily assembled grand procession, followed by the fire department in full force. Next came the druggist's wagon with its painted mortar and pestle, then the Vedders' grocery wagon sporting a long banner, the hand-lettered words proclaiming, *"We have peppered the Rebs 'til they cried 'Peas!'"*

A brass band played aboard a wagon, and Teddy saluted the Veterans' Reserve Corps marching past. Railroad workers blowing tin horns added to the din. Near the end of the parade, Hattie and Teddy waved their flags high for the Fifty-first Wisconsin, a regiment with a full company of artillery, guns, and caissons.

Father stood with his hat in his hand. "I'd rather see weapons in a parade than on a battlefield."

That evening as the full moon rose, the Bigelow household walked downtown together, Hattie and Teddy in the lead, Mother and Father arm in arm, followed by Ellen and Mr. Jenkins. Hattie glanced over her shoulder and smiled. "We're the Bigelow Brigade."

They arrived at the riverbank just as the first firework whistled into the air and exploded into a bright chrysanthemum in the night sky.

"I don't understand why Miss Taft stayed home," Hattie said to Mr. Jenkins. "We won the war. This is the greatest day ever!"

"It's a mystery," he replied. "But I'm glad you and I can celebrate this day together."

Hattie turned to him and saw the shops and businesses illuminated in the moonlight. This was the same spot, she realized, where she had stood the night of the torchlight procession on Election Eve. Her face clouded over for a moment. Then she took off her rosette and pinned it on his lapel.

28.

THAT SATURDAY MORNING Hattie pattered down the
stairs in her stocking feet, lured by the smell of
bacon wafting from the kitchen. The entire week had felt
like a holiday, even at school when Miss Taft tried to con-
vince the students to attend to their lessons. Tomorrow the
church bells would peal to celebrate both Easter Sunday
and the end of the war.

A sharp rapping startled her. Before she could leave
the staircase, Mr. Jenkins hurried to the door from the
dining room, cup in hand.

A stranger's voice said, "Have you heard the news from
Washington?"

Mr. Jenkins nodded.

"He died this morning," said the stranger. "God help
us all."

The door closed.

Hattie whispered, "Who died?"

Mr. Jenkins set his teacup on the marble shelf of the
hall tree. Slowly he unpinned the rosette from his lapel
and placed it beside the cup. "President Lincoln was shot
last night at a theater."

Hattie clung to the stair rail, staring at the bright
rosette on the black marble. She could think of nothing to
say. What did a person do upon hearing such news?

An hour later she and Teddy walked to the shop with Father. Though many people seemed to be wandering the streets, an eerie quiet hung in the air. Even the newsboys were silent, simply holding up the papers with the stark headlines instead of shouting out the news. Near the telegraph office a crowd waited to hear the latest from Washington. Women dabbed their cheeks with black-edged handkerchiefs. One man sat on a bench with his head in his hands, shoulders heaving as he wept. Hattie slipped her hand into Father's and looked up to see tears glistening in his eyes.

Father unlocked the door of the shop and removed the tricolored wreath. Once inside, Hattie and Teddy walked to the display window and began pulling flags from the polished boots and laced-up brogans. All along East Water Street, men were pulling down the red, white and blue bunting and draping black in its place.

On a wet afternoon the following week, Hattie and Mother sat in the front room at the Soldiers' Home stitching black armbands onto blue jackets while Mrs. Buttrick and the matron assisted soldiers who were dressing in the back room. Every man not completely bedridden was determined to be in uniform for President Lincoln's funeral.

Private Mackenzie, keeping watch at the front door, called to Mrs. Buttrick. "Your carriage is here, ma'am."

"Go on without me, please. Those of you who are able may ride in the procession."

Private Mackenzie held his kepi over his heart where the empty sleeve was pinned. "I beg your pardon, ma'am, but the men will want to see you pay your respects, with your husband the Colonel and all." The other soldiers murmured agreement.

Mrs. Buttrick sighed. "I would dearly love to do so, but there are ill men upstairs."

Hattie looked at the somber soldiers. "Missus Buttrick, if Mother cares for the men upstairs, I'll stay down here with the others."

"But don't you want to see the procession?"

"I'll watch here with the soldiers."

"Are you sure?" Mrs. Buttrick glanced at Mother.

"Please go, Fanny," Mother said. "Hattie and I will manage just fine."

Private Mackenzie crooked his elbow to escort Mrs. Buttrick to the carriage.

"I'll go up and sit with the invalids," said Mother. "Will you be able to finish the armbands on the uniforms?"

Hattie nodded, needle in hand. With a few basting stitches she caught an armband in place on the right sleeve of a jacket. As soon as she finished one, another soldier handed her his jacket. She bent over the stitching until her neck ached and her finger hurt from pushing the needle through the heavy wool.

"That's the last of 'em," said Private Anderson, a one-legged soldier sitting near Hattie. "Thank you, miss." He checked the clock on the mantel. "The procession should be starting from the church now." He reached for his crutches so that he could hobble outside.

Hattie looked at the men in her charge. Simply getting out of bed and dressing had taxed some of them already. With help from one of the able-bodied men, Hattie maneuvered a bench from the dining table onto the front porch. Then she and the matron carried out chairs while the soldiers helped their comrades.

By the time all the men were seated on the porch, the funeral procession was only a few blocks away. It seemed strange to see the black-plumed horses pulling a hearse with an empty coffin inside. President Lincoln's body was still in Washington. According to the newspapers, ceremonial funeral events like the one in Milwaukee were taking place in all of the Northern states.

On this gray morning the black bunting on the buildings and the drab clothing of the mourners made the street look like a photograph. Hattie wore her dark-blue dress without its white lace collar and cuffs. The brass buttons on the soldiers' uniforms seemed to be the only glimmer of light in the dreary world.

As the hearse approached, the soldiers rose shakily to their feet. Private Anderson, the soldier with one leg, looked wildly about for his crutches, which were nowhere to be seen.

"Let me help." Hattie slipped her shoulder under his arm and braced herself while he tottered to stand. Tears stung her eyes as the men saluted their fallen leader, and she remembered that only last week Colonel Buttrick had been planning a grand victory parade.

29.

A WEEK LATER, HATTIE GAZED with satisfaction at the freshly turned soil in her garden, which now stretched almost to the back fence. She thanked Jerry, the handyman, who tipped his cap and went whistling back to St. Gall's.

As she was breaking up clods of dirt with a hoe, Teddy called from the porch. "Would you like to play ball? You've never tried my bat."

Hattie shook her head. "We're behind on planting, and I still need to make a delivery."

"I'll hoe the garden while you go to the Soldiers' Home. Then we'll have time to play."

Hattie blinked. "Thank you, Teddy."

When Hattie arrived at the back door of the Soldiers' Home with her wagonload of withered beets and carrots, the last of the previous year's crop from the root cellar, she met Mrs. Buttrick stepping down from the unpainted porch. "Hattie Bigelow, you're an answer to prayer. Run and fetch Missus Moores for me, please."

"Charlie's mother?" Hattie stared at Mrs. Buttrick's red-rimmed eyes and dropped the handle of the wagon. "Is Charlie here?"

"He arrived on the train last evening, but has taken a

turn for the worse. Please run to fetch his mother."

Hattie brushed past Mrs. Buttrick and opened the door. "Let me see him first."

Mrs. Buttrick caught her arm. "He's ill with the fever. You shouldn't be here."

"But he's my friend! What if . . . what if something happens?"

Mrs. Buttrick let go of her, and Hattie entered the building and made her way to the sleeping quarters. She recognized the dark curls on the pillow before she knew the face with its closed eyes and slightly open mouth.

Pulling up a low stool, she said softly, "Charlie? It's Hattie. Hattie Bigelow."

The eyelids fluttered open, but he did not seem to see her. "Hattie—what are you doing here? Joined up, have you?"

"No, Charlie. We're in Milwaukee. You've come home." Hattie brushed a damp tendril from his forehead.

Charlie stared at the ceiling. "Milwaukee? But the war—I have to get back to the regiment. We look after one another—we're a team." He struggled to raise himself from the pillow.

"No, Charlie, the war is over. We won, remember?"

"That's right," he murmured, settling back. "We celebrated in camp—before I took ill."

Missus Buttrick laid a cool cloth on the furrowed brow. "That's right, Charlie. And now you're at the Soldiers' Home, and soon your mother will be here."

"Missus Buttrick is looking after you, Charlie. She'll get you back on your feet."

130

He managed a faint smile. "Missus Buttrick. She's a gallant lady." Then he fell silent, panting slightly.

"Only a few minutes, Hattie," whispered Mrs. Buttrick. She turned toward another bed and spoke soothingly to a fretful young soldier.

Hattie took Charlie's clammy hand in hers. "I'm glad you've come home. Your mother will be so glad to see you." She attempted to keep her voice as calm and steady as Mrs. Buttrick's, but she had to clench her jaw to keep from crying.

Charlie murmured, "You're much like her, you know."

"Like your mother?"

He moved his head slowly side to side. "Like Missus Buttrick."

Hattie could think of nothing to say.

Charlie closed his eyes, and as he spoke, Hattie watched the long damp lashes on the pale cheek. "Down in Memphis, during Forrest's raid, all of us green soldiers were shaking in our shoes. Not Missus Buttrick. She was steady as a rock—always looking after others—never a thought about herself."

"Oh, Charlie. I'm nothing like that. Sometimes all I think about is myself."

"Remember the sleighing party—the soldiers' families? Your garden—and now the Fair. Dear Hattie—I'm glad you're on my team."

Hattie smiled as the tears rolled down her face. "I am, too." She heard the rustling of Mrs. Buttrick's skirts. "I—I must go now." Gently she laid his hand on the scarlet coverlet and whispered. "Farewell."

Charlie's hand reached out frantically.

Immediately she grasped it in both of hers. "What is it, Charlie?"

The lashes fluttered, and his eyes met hers as last. "You'll teach my sisters, won't you? To be like you."

Hattie's throat was so tight she could barely speak. "Yes, Charlie." Her tears spotted the coverlet as she leaned to kiss his fingers.

Mrs. Buttrick stepped over and laid her hand on Charlie's forehead. "Quickly now."

Blindly, Hattie stumbled out of the room, pushed open the back door, and ran for home.

30.

A T FOREST HOME CEMETERY the gnarled oak branches, their tiny green leaves barely unfurled, towered
above Charlie's grave, a dark hole in the ground. Alongside
the stack of newly cut turf, Hattie stood with Mother and
Father, Teddy, Ellen, and Mr. Jenkins. Mrs. Moore kept her
black veil lowered. In their white dresses trimmed with
black ribbon, Molly and Bea made their mother's mourning dress seem even blacker.

Though Hattie's run had brought Mrs. Moores to
Charlie's side in time to say goodbye, she knew his sisters
had been kept away, for fear that they might take ill.

The bugler began a cadence of notes that echoed over
the rolling hills. After the last note sounded, Charlie's
mother stepped forward to drop the first handful of dirt
into the grave. Her fist clutched the dirt for a moment as
the hand shook, and then she opened her hand as gently as if she were releasing a butterfly. Others stepped
forward, and as clods of dirt rattled onto the pine coffin,
Molly and Bea sobbed louder and louder. Hattie buried her
face in her mother's embrace as if she were no older than
the Moores girls.

All afternoon visitors called to offer their condolences
at the house with the black crepe wreath on the door. After

the Bigelows returned home, Hattie wandered blindly into the back yard and found the hoe where Teddy had dropped it when she had told him about Charlie.

Charlie—who would never again stand at home plate with a confident smile. Charlie—who would never again see the moon rise over the lilacs.

Hattie picked up the hoe and swung it savagely at the ground, slicing a clod of dirt. Another vicious blow, and another. She struck the earth again and again. The back door creaked open. "Darlin', you needn't be doing that. We can hire one of the St. Gall's men to finish it."

Hattie did not respond. The sound of metal slicing dirt became a rhythm that filled the world.

"Hattie Bigelow."

The voice at the gate commanded such power that Hattie stood still, not lifting her eyes to look at Miss Taft.

"I know what it means to lose a loved one to war. I know how it feels to grieve the senseless waste of a young life."

Hattie looked up at that, but the teacher's gaze was fixed on the house next door.

"I have found little consolation in words, so I have none to offer," said Miss Taft. "Work has helped me make my way through the darkness. I hope to see you and Teddy and George in school on Monday." The gate clicked shut, and the firm footsteps clicked up the porch steps.

At last Hattie dropped the hoe, peered at her blistered hands, and rubbed her stiff fingers. A breeze rustled the leaves and a robin chirped on the fence. Hattie remembered how she had longed for color in a city draped in black. Now the sunlit springtime seemed to mock her.

How dare the flowers bloom, when Charlie was dead? How dare the sun rise and set and the moon continue waxing and waning? The world continued to turn as if nothing were different—yet nothing under the sun and moon would ever be the same.

From the corner of the yard, Teddy and George walked slowly to the porch and sat on the bottom step, so close that their knees touched. Teddy clutched his base ball and gazed silently at the garden. After a moment Hattie realized that he was staring at home base.

At the faint sound of a slamming door she turned toward the Moores house. Through the opening in the hedge Molly and Bea ran through the lilacs, their faces red and contorted above their white dresses. They disappeared like rabbits deep into the bushes, and Hattie could hear them sobbing. She crept through the new growth to sit beside the girls huddled beneath the oldest lilac. Bea climbed onto her lap and pressed her face against Hattie's shoulder. "Mama won't let me carry my parasol with the pink ribbons."

Molly sniffled. "She said if we wear pretty colors, people will think we didn't love Charlie. She's going to wear a black dress for a whole year."

Hattie wished that the girls' black crepe bows did not remind her of the wreath on their front door. "That's what women do when they're in mourning."

There was a rustling of leaves as Teddy and George pushed through the lilacs to sit on either side of Hattie and Molly. For a little while all of the children were silent, breathing the fragrance of the earth as the birds chirped above them.

Bea eyed the ball in Teddy's hand. "Maybe Charlie is playing base ball in heaven. He could make a ball, like he did in Memphis."

Teddy swiped his fist across his eyes. "Charlie could do anything."

George murmured, "He was a good soldier."

Molly nodded. "He was the best brother ever."

"I don't want him to be in heaven!" wailed Bea. "I want him *here*."

"We all do," whispered Hattie, her tears falling onto Bea's dark curls.

May 1865

31.

DURING THE FOLLOWING WEEKS the Fourth Ward School was abuzz with excitement about various events connected with the Soldiers' Home Fair. Hattie paid little attention to the chatter of classmates as they waved official certificates indicating how many bricks they had purchased for the Soldiers' Home at ten cents a share. She took no interest in Principal Martin's announcement of a Fourth Ward School entertainment at Birchard's Hall. She stared at her desk while Miss Taft explained the selections for the sixth grade performances and Lizzie Eisenmenger immediately took charge. After school that day Hattie lingered in the classroom after the other students left.

"Miss Taft, I don't care to participate in the school entertainment."

"Hattie, you have such a forceful presence. The shy girls will perform better with you among them."

Hattie scowled. "I will not dress up like a flower and prance about the stage."

Miss Taft pursed her lips. "Very well. You may serve as wardrobe mistress."

Hattie blinked at the unexpected victory. "Thank you, Miss Taft."

Hattie crouched in the garden a week later, carving a shallow trench with the point of her trowel. Stooping behind her, Teddy dropped a bean every two inches. When Hattie saw George trotting through the lilacs, she straightened up. "Teddy can't stop to play until we finish planting the beans."

George stood at the edge of the garden. "I don't want to play. I want to work with you. Mother said we ought to have a garden, too. If I help you, will you teach me?"

Hattie stuck her trowel into the ground and showed George how to use both hands to cover the row of seeds and pat the dirt into place.

When the last row of beans was planted, George brushed dirt from his knees and asked, "Hattie, will you help me learn my lines?" He pulled a crumpled paper from his pocket. "Gus and I are going to be rival gladiators in ancient Rome."

Teddy looked smug. "I know all of my lines already."

Hattie rolled her eyes. "We *all* know your lines, Teddy. Go and stand on the other end of the garden so George can practice speaking for Birchard's Hall. George, pick up one of those garden stakes. You'll feel more like a gladiator if you hold a sword."

With the script for "The Rival Gladiators" in one hand and her trowel in the other, Hattie intoned, "*We meet again,*" in a deep, dramatic voice.

George mumbled, "*But not, I hope, in anger.*"

"Try to sound like a warrior," said Hattie. "Be strong and bold."

After George recited his closing lines, Teddy's applause was joined by Molly's and Bea's. The two little girls had slipped unnoticed into the yard to sit at the edge of the garden.

"Will you practice with me again tomorrow, Hattie?" George stuck the picket back into the ground. "I wanted to have a swordfight, but my teacher said the country's had enough fighting."

"Hattie!" called Molly. "Mama said we can go for an outing this afternoon if we find someone to take us."

"Mama never goes anywhere except to church," sighed Bea, swinging a little black bag by its strings. "I want to go to the Fair!"

"The Fair doesn't open till the end of June," George said. "The workmen are still constructing the building."

Bea clapped her hands. "I want to see the building!"

The Moores girls ended up riding in Teddy's wagon, which the boys pulled like a team of horses while Hattie walked alongside.

As they approached the river, Molly waved to passersby and Bea dangled her black drawstring bag over the side of the wagon, letting it swing just above the sidewalk. The boys were panting by the time they crossed the bridge. The screeching of gulls was punctuated by the rhythm of hammers echoing off brick walls.

Beyond the storefronts on East Water Street rose the gigantic framework of the Fair building. The beams and rafters of the roofless central hall towered high above the broad wings on either side. The new wood shone like gold in the afternoon light, and the Stars and Stripes flew at the very peak. Workmen in the rafters were silhouetted against billowing white clouds and brilliant blue sky.

"It's beautiful," breathed Molly.

"It looks like heaven," said Bea.

Beside the wide doorway into the central hall, two workmen were nailing battens onto the outer wall boards. Hammer in hand, one of them paused to look at the children. "Sure, and if it isn't the little captain and his first mate. I remember you two and that wagon." He whistled a few bars of "My Bonnie Lies over the Ocean."

The other man grinned. "They've brought the entire crew today."

The friendly words gave Hattie the courage to ask, "May we please go inside?"

"No, I shouldn't like for anyone to drop a hammer on you. Still, you're welcome to stand at the door and take a peek."

"Thank you, sir!" Hattie had hardly spoken the words before Molly and Bea scrambled out of the wagon and trotted toward the doorway, followed by the boys.

George gaped at the vast interior. "Birchard's Hall doesn't seem so big anymore."

"This is as big as our whole block," said Teddy. "Plenty of room for playing ball."

"I've got Charlie's base ball," said Bea. She held up the black bag. "Mama lets me carry it to remember him."

The first workman looked at Bea, then turned to Hattie. "Are those the Moores girls?"

Hattie nodded.

"My boys were in school with young Charlie." He cleared his throat. "I do believe the men are about to take a break. Would you all like to toss that ball around inside?"

"Yes, sir!"

He whistled sharply to the men in the rafters and gave a quick command. Then he beckoned the children over the threshold.

Bea pulled out the base ball, and Molly called, "Throw it to me!"

Before Bea tossed the ball, she gazed up into the rafters framing the sky. "I think Charlie will be glad we're getting better at throwing."

Hattie's eyes stung.

After she caught Molly's throw, she tilted her head back to send the ball sailing high into the rafters. "For you, Charlie," she whispered as Teddy and George raced to catch it at the far end of the hall.

32.

O N A WARM EVENING Hattie supervised the wardrobe table backstage at Birchard's Hall. As other children whispered and squealed about missing props, scratchy costumes, and the terrifying prospect of forgetting their lines, she stood beside the fourth-grade teacher handing out wreaths and sashes.

Miss Beale checked her program anxiously. "The Flowers are to line up after the Revolutionary Fathers." She glanced at the table, where a coarse tunic and leather sandals lay beside a helmet and a tin sword. "And the other gladiator had best put on his gear."

One gladiator stood beside the table, already in costume. Hattie hardly recognized George under the helmet, but the glum voice was unmistakable. "Gus isn't coming. His sister says he's ill and was kept at home."

"Whatever will we do?" cried Miss Beale.

"Cut the gladiator scene, of course," said Lizzie Eisenmenger.

Hattie glared at her, but Lizzie was intent on smoothing the rose petals of her skirt.

"But I worked so hard to learn my part," said George.

As Miss Beale attempted to console him, and Lizzie began giving commands to the Flowers, Hattie snatched up the gladiator's gear. In the darkness behind the back curtain she kicked off her shoes, stripped off her stockings, unbuttoned her dress, and stepped out of her petticoats. She pulled the tunic over her shift and laced the leather sandals up her bare legs. Then she tucked her hair up inside the helmet and picked up the sword.

She found George in the dimly lit wings, still in costume. "You came!" he said in delight.

Miss Beale shushed him and whispered, "Hurry into place, boys."

The two gladiators waited in the wings on opposite sides of the stage. Beyond the edge of the curtain Hattie could see that the audience filled the hall. Almost everybody she knew must be here tonight. Hattie gripped her sword tightly and nodded to George. Illuminated by the gaslights, the rival gladiators stepped out onto the stage.

"*We meet again,*" said the first gladiator in a solemn tone.

"*But not, I hope, in anger,*" responded the other.

They continued their dialogue, ending with the rivals agreeing to flee the Roman arena and return to their own countries to live peaceful lives. After their closing lines, the gladiators bowed to the audience. Above the applause, Miss Beale called to them to take off their helmets for another bow.

Hattie pulled off the helmet and stood with sword in hand.

Abruptly the clapping stopped. Miss Beale caught her breath, and a murmur arose in the hall. Hattie caught George's eye and they bowed in unison. A deep voice shouted "Bravo!" and that one word from Colonel Buttrick triggered a hearty round of applause.

A week later Hattie and a dozen of the other Fourth Ward students ate teacakes and ginger cookies and drank ice-cold lemonade from crystal punch cups in the Buttricks' dining room. Colonel Buttrick had invited them to reprise their performances at a small gathering because his wife had been at the Soldiers' Home during the Birchard's Hall entertainment.

Mrs. Buttrick said to Mr. Van Vechten, "Even before the opening day of the Fair, I intend to feed every soldier who comes through Milwaukee."

Mr. Van Vechten chuckled. "When you ladies put your minds to something, it's as good as done. I remember hearing Missus Hewitt declare, 'I will have a soldiers' home in Milwaukee and will not stop until it is an accomplished fact.' Within a month the Soldiers' Home was open for business."

Colonel Buttrick raised his glass. "Gentlemen, I propose a toast to the ladies of the West Side."

"To the ladies!" chorused the men.

Mr. Van Vechten caught Hattie's eye. "You must be the Bigelow girl. Jim Jenkins tells me you're a base ball fan."

"I certainly am, sir."

"Many of our Wisconsin soldiers learned the game from the eastern regiments, where base ball has been popular for years. So we ought to have plenty of new fans. You tell Jenkins I said we're looking forward to seeing the Milwaukee Cream Citys take the field this summer."

"Yes, sir!"

After finishing their refreshments Hattie, George, and the other children donned their costumes. The short tunic brushing against her bare knees seemed out of place in a drawing room. If anyone other than Mrs. Buttrick had asked Hattie to reprise her role as a gladiator, Hattie doubted that Mother would have approved.

As she and George waited their turn, he groaned and adjusted his helmet. "I shouldn't have eaten so much. Did you see how many people are out there?"

"Don't think about the audience," said Hattie, more to herself than to him. "Be a warrior, strong and bold."

They both remembered all of their lines. Afterwards, during the first bow, one of the visiting soldiers rose to his feet, applauding furiously and whistling through his teeth.

George took off his helmet, but instead of bowing again, he dropped his sword suddenly and left Hattie alone as he pushed past billowing skirts to the back of the room, where the cheering soldier clutched him in a fierce embrace.

"Welcome home, Sergeant Schaefer," said Mrs. Buttrick from her seat in the front row.

Hattie picked up George's forgotten sword.

June 1865

33.

O N AN UNCOMFORTABLY HOT MORNING, Hattie pulled the wagon down the sidewalk toward the Soldiers' Home. Ellen had laid damp dish towels over the fresh lettuce to keep it from wilting, and Hattie wished she could wrap the towels around her own sweaty forehead. As she walked, Teddy's base ball bumped her from the pocket of the pinafore she had forgotten to take off before leaving home. Sergeant Schaefer had broken up the children's game of catch by asking Teddy to help him and George in their new garden.

Hattie turned into the alley and halted the wagon beside the porch piled with crates and bushel baskets. So accustomed to going in and out of the Soldiers' Home that she no longer knocked, she carried her bundle of lettuce and a small sack of fresh peas through the back door. Once inside, she delivered her greens to the kitchen. No one was about—the matron must be upstairs, and these days the lady managers were constantly running errands in preparation for the coming Fair.

Suddenly Hattie heard a shout, a crash, and a curse.

The commotion was in the main room. Without thinking she dashed past the rows of beds toward the front door. Beside the pieces of a broken lamp in the sitting room stood a soldier, with a rifle.

He swung around and pointed the bayonet at her. He stood just few steps away from the door.

"Who goes there? Don't move now." The soldier's voice was rough, his breath ragged. "Don't nobody move," he snarled, the rifle sweeping back and forth as he looked quickly around the large room. Then he fixed his gaze again on Hattie.

Pressed back against the wall, Hattie stared at the gleaming blade.

He glared at her, eyes wild. "Are you a Reb?"

"No, sir," Hattie whispered.

"You look like a Reb," he insisted, his voice full of suspicion. "Maybe you're a Rebel spy."

In desperation Hattie grabbed for the front door handle, but the soldier lunged forward and thrust the bayonet into the wood, pinning the door shut.

"Thought you'd get away, did you?"

Hattie shook her head. She opened her mouth, but no sound came out.

"Step away from the door."

She sidled toward the large front window. Where was the matron? Where was *anybody*?

The soldier wrenched the rifle from the door, but the bayonet remained stuck in the wood.

Thumping footsteps on the stairs brought Private Mackenzie to the main room. Surprise flickered only a moment over his face. "I'm here to relieve you, Ned." Calmly he approached the other soldier, reaching out his hand. "I'll keep watch now. Let me take the rifle."

Hattie slowly let out her breath as Ned lowered the rifle and relaxed his grip, reversing the weapon as if to give it to the other man. Suddenly Ned's head jerked up and he seized the barrel with both hands, swinging the rifle so violently that the butt sent Private Mackenzie staggering.

"No self-respectin' soldier would come on duty without 'is rifle," Ned snarled. "You must be a stinkin' Rebel too. I'll keep my own watch." His eyes darted around the room as he swung the butt of the rifle from side to side, his feet firmly planted.

What would Mrs. Buttrick do? With a shuddering breath Hattie wiped her sweaty hands on her pinafore. Her fingers curled around the base ball in her pocket.

She tried to speak, but again, no words came out until she remembered her own advice to George. Taking the base ball out of her pocket, she stood like a warrior, strong and bold. "Ned," she called, holding up the ball, "can you hit this?"

She drew back her arm and pitched the ball.

Without a moment's pause, Ned swung hard. The rifle butt thwacked the leather-covered ball with a full stroke, and Hattie ducked just in time as the ball shot past her head.

Crash!

As the large front window rained glass inside the room and out on the porch, Ned groaned and dropped the rifle.

He sank to the floor with his head in his hands.

Hattie scrambled through the splintered glass on hands and knees. She reached the rifle before Private Mackenzie did and pushed it across the floor to him.

Ned rocked back and forth, his voice choking with sobs. "I didn't mean to do it. I never meant to hurt no one."

No longer afraid, Hattie knelt beside him and said gently, "It's all right, sir. Nobody's hurt."

Above them Private Mackenzie said gruffly, "Nobody's hurt, Ned, but you had no business frightening folks like that. Let me help you there, Miss Hattie."

She grasped the hand he offered, then winced and let go. Turning up her palms, she found them covered in blood.

34.

HATTIE KNELT IN THE GARDEN beside George. "These are the carrots," she told him, pointing to the green fringe of seedlings with her bandaged hand. "You can tell by the lacy leaves. All the other ones are weeds. Pull 'em out."

"Lacy leaves, leave them be," called Teddy from the radishes.

"*Let* them be." Hattie smiled as she inspected the neat rows. Her fingers itched to get back to the soil, but Mother had forbidden that until her cuts healed.

From the porch Ellen called, "In with you now—Miss Taft tells me 'tis time for the Fair! Mind you wash up well, boyo."

Sitting on the bench in the back hall, Hattie fumbled with the laces of her work boots.

"Whist, none of that now. I'm the one to do that." Ellen knelt and pulled off Hattie's muddy boots.

Hattie sighed. "I hate not being able to do things for myself."

Deftly Ellen laced up Hattie's new shoes. "'Tis only for a week or two. Think of the poor boys who came back without an arm or a leg."

Hattie nodded. "I always do."

Hattie and Teddy found it difficult to slow their steps to Miss Taft's sedate pace as they approached the crowd lined up for the opening of the Soldiers' Home Fair. As they turned in their tickets and stepped inside the great Fair building, Hattie gazed in astonishment at the splendor disguising once-bare planks and beams. The rafters where she had thrown the base ball were crisscrossed with evergreen garlands, festooned with bunting, and hung with battle flags.

Above the gallery on the back wall stretched a huge banner proclaiming that *"The Only Debt We Can Never Repay is the Debt We Owe Our Union Soldiers."* On one side of the banner hung a portrait of George Washington labeled "Our Father," and on the other a portrait of Lincoln labeled "Our Savior."

Straight ahead rose the Floral Temple, entwined in greenery and adorned with pale statues of classically draped women. Only one decoration on the graceful gazebo did not fit the classical theme—a black-draped placard bearing a shield of Stars and Stripes and the single word *LINCOLN*.

"Welcome to the Fair!" Mrs. Buttrick called from an archway of the temple. Eagerly she answered Miss Taft's questions about the great number of exhibits and the expected income from donations and sales. Inside the floral gazebo, surrounded by pails of flowers, Lizzie Eisenmenger was in charge of the girls making tussie-mussies.

Hattie held out her bandaged hands to Mrs. Buttrick. "I'm sorry I can't be more help."

Lizzie glanced up from the stems she was wrapping with ribbon.

"Dear Hattie," Mrs. Buttrick said, "the soldiers have not stopped talking about the young lady who disarmed the sentry." Solemnly she presented a tussie-mussie. "For gallantry and devotion."

Hattie nodded her thanks and sniffed the fragrant Sweet William among the trailing ivy. "And friendship. Lizzie, this is beautiful."

Lizzie looked at her in surprise. "Why, thank you, Hattie."

At Mrs. Buttrick's suggestion, Hattie and Teddy climbed the stairs of the Floral Temple to watch the grand entrance of a returning regiment. Miss Taft chose to remain below.

Standing on a platform near the main doors as a fanfare from a brass band summoned the attention of the fairgoers, Mrs. Buttrick declared to the soldiers assembled in formation, "We welcome you home. Please proceed to the dining hall for a dinner, in thanks for your service." The crowd cheered, the band struck up "When Johnny Comes Marching Home," and a long line of blue-uniformed soldiers marched two by two through the central hall.

When Hattie and Teddy descended the stairs of the Floral Temple, Miss Taft had been joined by Miss Beale. The teachers agreed to meet them at an attraction called Tangle's Features in an hour.

Eagerly the children set off to explore the many wonders of the Fair, upstairs and down in the vast hall. They admired sparkling gems in glass cases and intricate clockworks in an assortment of timepieces. An orchestra played waltzes as they toured a natural history exhibit featuring a huge aquarium of exotic fish in jewel-bright colors.

In a side gallery they watched a glassblower form a crimson blob of molten glass into a brilliant cranberry vase.

When they discovered a miniature of the Monitor chugging down a long trough of water, Teddy was fascinated by the workings of the steam engine inside the glass model of the "ironclad" ship.

"Miss Hattie!" Private Mackenzie beckoned from near the agricultural manufacturing exhibit.

"Good day, Private Mackenzie. Are you enjoying the Fair?"

"I am," he said. "How are your hands?" he asked, taking one of her bandaged palms in his. "You'll be glad to know that Ned O'Brien finally understands the war is over." He grinned. "If we'd had you down South, we'd have won the war sooner."

Hattie smiled. "Armed with a base ball?"

One of the exhibitors called to Teddy, "Young man, have you ever shelled corn?"

Before Teddy could answer, the man reached out to hand him an ear of corn and pointed to a tin pail beside a small curious machine, equipped with a large flywheel.

Teddy grabbed the corn firmly and began to pop kernels off the end of the cob with his thumb, one by one.

As the kernels rattled in the pail, other fairgoers stopped to watch.

The man said, "Tough work, isn't it?"

Teddy nodded.

Private Mackenzie raised his hand. "Especially if you have only one arm."

"Or bandaged hands," added Hattie.

The man pointed to the machine. "Now your troubles are over. Behold the latest corn sheller—so simple a child can use it."

He handed Hattie an ear of corn. "Here, missy, feed this right in there. Soldier, turn that wheel, if you please."

Hattie dropped the ear of corn into a wooden chute. Then, Private Mackenzie cranked the wheel. The flywheel turned, the machine clattered, and yellow kernels rattled into the tin pail in a sharp rapid-fire stream. A few moments later, the empty cob fell out of another chute, landing at Hattie's feet.

The crowd murmured in amazement, and a grizzled farmer stepped forward to examine the machine.

Private Mackenzie said slowly, "Maybe I could go back to farming with my brother after all."

Hattie nodded. "I think you could do just about anything."

By the time she and Teddy joined Miss Taft and Miss Beale in the long line to buy tickets to Tangle's Features, the special menagerie tent outside the Fair building, Hattie had seen more new sights in one day than in her entire life before the Soldiers' Home Fair.

Teddy paid for the tickets with money Father had given them. The children ran from one cage to another, marveling over foxes and badgers, raccoons and spotted fawns, cranes and hawks. They pushed through the crowd to see the main attraction high on a perch. There sat Old Abe, the magnificent bald eagle that had gone to war with the Eighth Wisconsin regiment.

Carefully counting out the coins, Teddy bought souvenir picture cards of Old Abe for himself and Hattie.

Miss Beale said farewell to them at Jacob's Well. There, the children and Miss Taft were served lemonade by young women in Biblical attire with patriotic red and blue trim on their white robes. As Hattie and Teddy drank their cold, tangy lemonade, they admired the stuffed owls high on top of a star-spangled canopy swathed in mysterious veils. Beside a sign proclaiming the powers of the Delphic Oracle, fairgoers waited to have their fortunes told.

Teddy looked at Hattie. "Are you going to consult the Delphic Oracle?"

Miss Taft raised her eyebrows. "There's no scientific evidence to support such predictions."

Hattie smiled. "And Ellen would say 'tis bad luck to seek to know the future."

Teddy returned his empty glass to the women at the Well. "We haven't seen the war trophies yet."

Miss Taft grimaced, then said stiffly, "Very well."

Teddy led the way to the display of captured artifacts below a row of tattered Confederate regimental flags. He lingered over the long table piled with rifles and monogrammed pistols and engraved swords and bullet cases captured from the Southern troops. Hattie's throat tightened as she saw the Stars and Bars painted on a shattered drum.

155

Beside her, Miss Taft murmured, "I can hardly bear to look at these things," then drew in her breath sharply as she stared at the torn flag of the Tennessee Volunteers.

"What is it, Miss Taft?"

The teacher looked down and was silent. When at last she spoke, her voice trembled. "My cousins belonged to that regiment."

Hattie blinked. "You have family in the South?"

Miss Taft fumbled for her handkerchief. "I still think of Benjamin and Robert as the little brothers of the favorite cousin I visited every summer. Some years they all came north for the holidays." She dabbed at her nose. "I last saw them the Christmas after South Carolina seceded."

Hattie hesitated. "What happened to them?"

"Rob was killed at Chickamauga. Ben was taken prisoner. Nobody has heard from him."

"I'm so sorry," said Hattie, her eyes stinging. "Why didn't you ever tell us?"

"I didn't want anyone to think me a Confederate sympathizer." Miss Taft's mouth was a grim line. "I have always supported the Union."

She put her fingers to her lips and reached up to touch a ragged corner of the flag of the Tennessee regiment. "But I loved my cousins, too."

July 1865

35.

"I WOULD COME TO THE FAIR every day if I could," said Hattie as she, Teddy, and Mother entered the central hall one afternoon.

Mother quickened her pace. "Some of us work here so often it feels like every day."

Hattie looked at her clumsy bandaged hands. "I'm afraid the Fair will be over by the time I can help in the Floral Temple."

"Maybe not. The Fair is such a success that we are extending it two more weeks."

Teddy grinned. "Two more weeks of doughnuts!"

"I'll see you after my shift." Mother turned toward the dining hall. "We're to meet your father at the Holland Kitchen at five."

"Let's get doughnuts now," Teddy said.

Hattie rolled her eyes. "Missus Van Vechten fries a barrel of doughnuts every day, and you must eat half of them. I don't want to wait in line."

"Then let's each go our own way. See you at five." Teddy

trotted off toward one of his favorite spots at the fair, the kitchen serving the sweet Dutch doughnuts.

Hattie gloried in having the afternoon to herself. She strolled through the Fine Arts exhibit and examined the schoolchildren's crafts. In the wool department she admired gigantic piles of fleeces, dark and light and spotted, donated by farmers all over the state.

Two little girls in white dresses with black bows ran their hands over the soft fleeces. A black drawstring bag swung from one girl's wrist.

"Molly! Bea!" Hattie called. "Good afternoon, Missus Moores," she added to the black-veiled woman beside them.

The girls threw their arms around Hattie. "D'you see?" Molly crowed. "Mother came with us today!"

Bea bobbed her head. "She said it was everyone's duty to support the Soldiers' Home Fair!" Then she clapped her hands. "Hattie, come and see President and Missus Lincoln."

"That's right," said Molly. "You *must* see the Lincoln portraits."

Hattie and Mrs. Moores took hands with Molly and Bea, who pulled them through the crowd to photographs of the Lincolns framed by hundreds of worsted flowers.

"Hattie, did you make all those flowers?" asked Bea.

"I never made that many." Hattie stepped closer to inspect the daisies and roses and violets. "But some of these are mine. No wonder I couldn't find them at the craft display."

Mrs. Moores reached into her bag and unwrapped a

black-edged handkerchief. "Did you make this one?"

Hattie stared at a crumpled purple daisy. "It looks like the one I gave to Charlie."

Mrs. Moores' fingers closed around the flower. "This was in his jacket pocket. I didn't know where it came from till now." She opened her hand. "I wonder whether you'd like to have it as a remembrance."

The purple daisy became blurry as Hattie touched it, but she managed to whisper, "I will never forget him."

Mrs. Moores' hand closed around hers. "That means more than you could know."

After leaving the Moores, Hattie wrapped the wire stem around her wrist, forming a daisy bracelet. Nothing else at the Fair could compare to the gift that Charlie Moores had kept with him until the end. She checked the time by the clock display, then wandered through exhibits of jewelry and clothing and hats for sale. When she found the boot and shoes department, she could not resist straightening up a row of brogans on a shelf.

Nearby a young clerk stammered to a gentleman, who was holding a boot and looking a little impatient, "I'm not sure why the price is so high, sir. You see, Mister Brown was to be in charge of the selling."

Hattie stepped forward. "Could I be of assistance?"

The clerk and the other man stared at her.

"May I?" Hattie took the boot in her bandaged hands. "This is a particularly rugged cowhide." She turned the boot over. "And the boot will wear longer because the sole is stitched, not pegged. The army prefers stitched brogans like these for our soldiers. If you prefer, we could try to find you a less expensive pegged boot."

The gentleman smiled. "No, I'd best take these. What's your name, little miss?"

She handed the boot to the clerk. "Hattie Bigelow."

The clerk blinked. "You do know shoes. Could you stay to help until Mister Brown arrives?"

As she moved from one customer to another, sizing them for brogans and recommending styles, Hattie forgot all about the other exhibits at the Fair. Many fairgoers who had no intention of buying shoes stopped to listen to the girl with bandaged hands explaining grades of leather and types of stitching.

During a brief lull Hattie noticed a soldier whose left sleeve was pinned to his uniform, like Private Mackenzie's. She walked up to him and said, "Now that the war is over, sir, you need a different type of shoe."

He snorted. "And what would you recommend, missy?"

"Congress gaiters."

Hattie picked up one from the shelf. "Men in Washington particularly like these. The leather comes well above the ankle, like a brogan, and the side elastic makes the shoe easy to put on. No laces to tie."

He took the shoe in his one hand and said slowly, "I could try a pair of those." He sat down and yanked at his laces to untie them.

Hattie set a pair of Congress gaiters beside him and stepped away. "You won't need help with these."

The one-armed soldier suddenly showed greater interest. He stepped forward, slipped his foot into the new shoe, and used the leather loop on the back to pull it on. He pulled on the other shoe, stood up, and walked a few paces back and forth. He smiled at Hattie. "I'll take them—and I'll wear them home."

Hattie picked up the soldier's discarded shoes. "Would you like us to wrap your old ones?"

"Give them to somebody who needs them." He walked over to the table to pay for his Congress gaiters.

"Hattie Bigelow!" Mother stood with her arms crossed. "Do you have any idea what time it is? Do you know how many people have been looking for you? How could you be so thoughtless?"

Before Hattie could respond, the clerk said, "It was my fault, Missus Bigelow. I never thought of the time or whether she ought to be doing such a thing. Hattie sold more shoes than I did—she's surely doing her part to support the Fair."

"And she certainly knows the business."

Hattie turned to see Father behind her.

"I saw you with that last customer," he said gruffly. "Well done, Hattie girl."

36.

ON INDEPENDENCE DAY, Mother draped a tri-colored sash over Hattie's shoulder, adjusted the rosette at her hip, and set a wreath of white daisies on her head. Then Hattie and Miss Taft set off to meet the other Fourth Ward girls who would ride on the Car of Liberty in the parade.

As they walked down Clybourn Avenue, Miss Taft said, "I received a note from Missus Buttrick yesterday." Her voice sounded odd. "Someone must have told her about my cousins in Tennessee."

Hattie stopped in mid-stride. "Oh, Miss Taft, I did tell Missus Buttrick—I thought she or the Colonel might be able to help—I'm so sorry." She struggled to catch up with the teacher, who was walking briskly toward the river.

"Missus Buttrick wrote to say that after the Colonel sent a number of telegrams, he learned that my cousin Ben, and some other men from his regiment, have been located in a prisoner of war camp at Camp Chase in Ohio. He should be home within the month." Now Miss Taft stopped abruptly. "Thank you, Hattie."

Hattie smiled, and she and Miss Taft continued down the street side by side.

The Car of Liberty was easy to spot in the lineup of parade wagons. Schoolgirls from each of the Milwaukee wards stood in noisy clusters around the tiered pyramid decked in patriotic bunting. Even the team of white horses wore tri-color rosettes on their bridles. The top tier of the Car of Liberty rose as high as the second floor of a building. A young woman portraying the Goddess of Liberty stood in the place of honor at the top.

The man supervising the boarding of the wagon said, "I'll need four brave girls to climb way up there."

Hattie stepped forward. "I volunteer, sir."

She and the other three climbed to the top tier, sitting down and arranging their skirts neatly around them. As other girls took their places on the lower tiers, Hattie pulled the purple worsted daisy from her pocket. A year ago Charlie Moores had celebrated Independence Day with his comrades at Camp Buttrick. Taking off her wreath, Hattie twisted the stem of the worsted flower among the fresh daisies, one spot of purple in a field of white.

That afternoon in the Bigelow back yard, Mr. Jenkins stood on the garden path with his shirt sleeves rolled up. Behind him Sergeant Schaefer, George, Teddy, and Bea lined up along the edge of the garden near the lilac hedge. Molly stood at the worn burlap base with the long bat resting on her small shoulder. Behind her, Hattie called softly, "Now, remember what I told you. Swing straight! Just meet the ball."

Mr. Jenkins gently lobbed Charlie's base ball toward Molly, who squealed when her slow but steady swing connected and sent the ball bouncing through the garden. On the porch Mother and Father, Mrs. Moores, Mrs. Schaefer, and Miss Taft applauded while Teddy and George fielded the ball from among the potatoes.

Hattie put her arm around Molly's shoulders. "I knew you would be a fine base ball player."

"Like Charlie?"

"Just like Charlie."

On the porch Mother opened the door for Ellen, who carried out a pan of custard for making ice cream. Father carried the churn down the steps, set it beside the rosebush and called "Which of you ball players will help churn ice cream?"

Molly and Bea were first in line, followed by Teddy and George, who tossed the ball back to Mr. Jenkins and headed for the porch.

Hattie looked down the garden path. "May I have a chance to strike? My hands are fine now."

Mr. Jenkins smiled. "Take your stance."

She picked up the bat.

Mr. Jenkins turned to Sergeant Schaefer. "Ready in the outfield?"

"Fire away!"

Hattie swung at the first pitch, connecting with a resounding thwack that sent the ball up over the lilacs.

"Well struck!" called Mother. "That could have been a home run."

Hattie tapped one black boot on the burlap bag. "I'm already home."

Historical Notes

"**T**HIS IS A STORY that needs to be told," our friend Patricia Lynch said one afternoon. "And you are the ones who can tell it." Patricia had first learned of Hattie in a letter that Fanny Buttrick, who accompanied the Thirty-ninth Wisconsin Infantry to Memphis in July 1864, wrote to her friend Lydia Hewitt back home in Milwaukee: *My love and many thanks to little Hattie Bigelow for her jar of beautiful jelly. It made me quite hungry to look at it.*"

So began our journey into the world of Hattie Bigelow and other Milwaukee children and women who did their part to support the Union cause during the Civil War.

Fanny Buttrick, Lydia Hewitt, Hannah Vedder, and Hattie's mother Harriet Bigelow were members of the West Side Soldiers' Aid Society, which became the Soldiers' Home Society in the spring of 1864 when the organization rented a storefront on West Water Street (now Plankinton Avenue) to provide housing and care for Wisconsin soldiers in Milwaukee.

Hattie's mother served as one of the volunteer managers of the Soldiers' Home, and her father owned a boot and shoe shop downtown. The Bigelow household included Irish housekeeper Ellen Carroll and two boarders—city attorney James G. Jenkins, who helped to found Milwaukee's first base-ball club, and Jemima Taft, a schoolteacher.

While the personalities of these characters are of our own making, the historical details are accurate. For example, to raise funds for the Soldiers' Home Fair, the children of the Fourth Ward School performed at Birchard's Hall. "The Rival Gladiators" was included in the program, but there is no record of a girl shedding her petticoats to become a gladiator!

In the summer of 1865 the great Soldiers' Home Fair raised over $100,000 to purchase land and build a permanent Soldiers' Home just west of Milwaukee. In 1867 the women of the Soldiers' Home Society turned their assets, including their Spring Street property, over to the federal government, facilitating the purchase of close to 400 acres for the Northwest Branch of the National Home for Disabled Volunteer Soldiers.

Nearly 150 years later, this property continues to serve soldiers and veterans as the grounds of the Clement J. Zablocki VA Medical Center. The original brick domiciliary, now known as Old Main, and other 19th-century buildings still stand in the National Soldiers Home Historic Landmark District.

The modern West Side Soldiers' Aid Society (www.wssas.org) raises funds for Wisconsin veterans' initiatives and conducts educational programs on the history and heritage of the Civil War years.

In 1864 the women of the Soldiers' Home Society also purchased cemetery plots for those soldiers who died without friends or family to bury them. Visitors to Forest Home Cemetery in Milwaukee can see the Soldiers' Home plot or leave a flower on the nearby grave of Charles Mooers (sic), the drummer boy who served in the Thirty-ninth Wisconsin and died of fever in Memphis.

❧

Further information and links to related resources are available online:
www.plankroad.wordpress.com

❧

Acknowledgements

We are grateful to Patricia Lynch, who introduced us to Hattie and conducted many hours of research on our behalf. In providing services to veterans, Patricia and her colleagues in the modern West Side Soldiers' Aid Society continue the work of the "gallant ladies" of 19th-century Milwaukee.

Many thanks to readers of early drafts of our story,

including James Marten of Marquette University, Don Driscoll, Louisa Ishida, Elena Lutze, Lynn Seep, Kathy Steffen and fellow novelists at Write by the Lake, and the Creative Writing students of Chesterton High School.

During our field research we enjoyed both history and hospitality with the Milwaukee Cream Citys Vintage Base-Ball Club, courtesy of Gary "Handlebar" Hetzel and Jeff "The Gent" Paige. We also appreciate the critical eye and keen insight of editor Philip Martin, who insisted that we keep working till we got the story right.

We thank our sister Gretchen Demuth Hansen for the cover photograph, along with Civil War re-enactor Faith Gorman, and the Anderson family of Yorkville, at whose home the photograph was taken.

As always, we thank the Lutzes of Hil-Mar Farm and the Ishidas of Spring Rose Cottage for their love and patience in putting up with the authors among them. Finally, of course, we owe more than we can say to our mother, Marjorie Demuth, who embodies the spirit of volunteerism that is the legacy of Wisconsin women past and present.

CPSIA information can be obtained at www.ICGtesting.com
Printed in the USA
LVOW12s0534241014

410229LV00001B/1/P

9 781883 953768